GREAT ILLUSTRATED CLASSICS

THE PHANTOM OF THE OPERA

Gaston Leroux

Adapted by
Shannon Donnelly
Illustrations by Robert Schoolcraft

BARONET BOOKS, New York, New York

GREAT ILLUSTRATED CLASSICS

edited by
Rochelle Larkin

Published by Playmore Inc., Publishers
230 Fifth Avenue, New York, N.Y. 10001
and Waldman Publishing Corp.
570 Seventh Avenue, New York, N.Y. 10018

Printed in the United States of America

Contents

About the Author

Gaston Louis Alfred Leroux was born in Paris on May 6, 1868, but only "by chance" as he later told others. "It was actually between trains—my parents were on a journey to my mother's home in Normandy," Leroux would say. He loved sailing and swimming. And he went to school in Normandy, France.

Leroux began to write stories at a young age. He studied to be a lawyer, but when his father died in 1889 and left him a million francs, Leroux quit his job. When the money was gone, Leroux took up a job as a reporter for *L'Echo de Paris*. He started by writing about court cases, and became famous by deciding to use fiction to solve a real crime—which he did.

In 1903, Leroux had his first novel published, *The Seeking of the Morning Treasures*. The story was based on a real robber from the early 1700s. Then *The Mystery of the Yellow Room* came out in 1907. Over the next two years Leroux made enough money to start writing novels full-time. He wrote plays and short stories as well.

In 1910 Leroux wrote *The Phantom of the Opera*. Leroux said he wrote the novel after visiting the real Paris Opera House and seeing the real underground lake there. Hollywood made the book into a movie in 1925, starring Lon Chaney.

Leroux died in Nice, France, on April 15, 1927, at the age of fifty-nine. His other books had never brought him great wealth, but *The Phantom of the Opera* made him famous as well.

The Great Paris Opera

CHAPTER 1

Is It the Ghost?

In Paris, there once was a time when everyone met at the Opera House. Fine carriages drawn by beautiful horses lined up before the huge stone building with its grand staircases and carpeted rooms, its vast stage, and the hundreds of hidden rooms behind the stage. Inside the Opera House, ladies in silk and diamonds and gentlemen in evening clothes strolled beneath gas-lit lamps, all as sparkling and rich as the theater itself.

So it was one evening, when the managers

of the Opera had planned a last grand show before they retired from their jobs.

Suddenly the dressing room of one of the chief dancers was invaded by six young girls of the ballet who had run upstairs from the stage. They rushed in, some almost crying in terror. Madam Sorelli, whose dressing room this was, looked around angrily at the girls.

"It's the ghost!" one girl told Madam Sorelli in a trembling voice.

Madam Sorelli shivered when she heard about the ghost. She called the girl a "silly little fool." But then she asked quietly, "Have you seen him?"

"As plainly as I see you now!"

"If that's the ghost, he's very ugly!" said Meg, another dancer.

"Oh, yes!" cried all the ballet girls. They all began to talk at once about the phantom they'd just seen. The ghost had appeared in the shape of a gentleman in black evening clothes,

"It's the Ghost!"

standing before them in the passageway. He seemed to have come straight through the wall!

"Pooh!" said one of them, who did not believe in ghosts. "You think you see the ghost everywhere!"

And it was true. For several months, there had been a great deal of talk at the Opera about a phantom who stalked the building like a shadow and who vanished as soon as he was seen. When the ghost did not show himself, he made his presence felt by causing accidents. Everything that happened, even a lost powder puff, was being blamed on the "Opera Phantom."

One man, the chief scene-changer, really had seen the ghost. He had run up against him on the stairs that led to the rooms under the Opera House. He had seen him for a second, and later reported: "He is thin and his coat hangs as if on a skeleton. His eyes are so deep that you just see two big black holes, as in a dead man's skull!"

ll!" Meg stammered.

The other girls kept at her and promised would keep the secret, too, until Meg, with eyes fixed on the door, said, "Well, it's use of the private box."

"What private box?"

"The Phantom's box!" Meg said.

"Has the ghost a private opera box? Oh, do us!" another dancer chimed in.

"Not so loud!" Meg said. "It's Box Five. You w, the box on the grand balcony, on the left. t's the ghost's box."

"And does the Phantom really come there?" d one girl, shivering.

"Yes. The ghost comes, but only when there obody there. You can only hear him when he his theater box. But we should not talk of se things. It will bring bad luck," Meg said.

Madam Sorelli turned pale. "I shall never be to give my speech to the managers before

"It is the ghost! The Opera Phantom!" one girl cried again to the other dancers. Silence fell in the dressing room. Then the girl, with terror on her face, whispered, "Listen!"

They seemed to hear a rustling outside the dressing-room door. There was no sound of footsteps. The rustling was like light silk brushing over the panel.

Then it stopped.

Madam Sorelli tried to show more courage than the others. She went to the door and asked, "Who's there?"

But nobody answered.

Feeling all eyes upon her, she made an effort not to show her fear, and said loudly, "Is there anyone behind the door?"

"Oh, yes, yes! Of course there is!" cried a girl named Meg, holding Madam Sorelli back by her skirt. "Whatever you do, don't open the door!"

But Madam Sorelli opened the door. The girls ran to the other side of the dressing room.

Madam Sorelli looked into the hall. It was

She Slammed the Door Closed.

empty. Only a gas lamp flickered wa
empty passage.

The chief dancer slammed the c
"No," she said, "there is no one ther

"Still, we saw him!" one girl sa
back to stand beside Madam Sorelli
be somewhere. We had better all go
together to hear the managers' speec
we will come up again together."

"Come, pull yourselves togethe
has ever really seen the ghost," Mad
said to the girls.

"Yes, yes, we saw him—we saw
now!" cried the girls. "He had a dea
and black clothes!"

No one said anything for a mome
Meg said, "Hush! Mother says the gho
like being talked about."

"And why does your mother say so
one asked.

"Because...because...nothing...I sw

"The Phantom's Box!" Meg Said.

they leave tonight," she complained.

She left her dressing room to go downstairs to the farewell party being given for the managers. The ballet girls followed right behind her, staying close to her and each other, clinging together as they crept fearfully downstairs and through the dark hall.

CHAPTER 2

The New Opera Star

Downstairs, Madam Sorelli met a nobleman she knew, Count Philippe. The count was very excited. "Madam Sorelli, what an evening! And Christine Daaé—how magnificently she sang tonight!" he said.

"Impossible!" said one of the dancers. "Six months ago, she squawked like a crow!" But that night at the Opera had been special. No other performance had been quite like it. All the great composers had led the orchestra in playing their greatest works.

The Audience Went Mad with Delight.

Christine Daaé, for the first time ever, had sung like an angel.

She had begun with a song from *Romeo and Juliet*. It was the first time anyone had sung that music at the Opera. And when the famous singer Madam Carlotta suddenly became ill, Christine sang the last part of the opera *Faust* in Madam Carlotta's place.

The whole audience went mad with delight, rising to its feet, shouting, cheering, and clapping. Overcome by this, Christine had fainted in the arms of the other singers and was quickly carried off the stage.

Count Philippe had applauded for Christine, too. He was from a proud, old noble family. He had two sisters and a brother named Raoul. The two sisters were married, but the count still watched after his younger brother, who was just twenty-one.

The count was proud of Raoul and arranged for him to be in the Navy, perhaps even one day becoming an admiral.

Just now, with Raoul on leave from the Navy, the count planned to show Raoul around Paris and tonight had brought Raoul to the Opera.

That evening, the count, after applauding for Christine, turned to Raoul and saw that he had turned pale. "What's the matter?" he asked.

Raoul just stood there. Then he said, "Let's go and meet Miss Daaé. She has never sung like that before."

They left their seats and made their way to the door that led to the stage. At the stage, they pushed through the crowd with Raoul leading the way.

Raoul felt that his heart was no longer even in his chest. He felt hollow. His brother, Count Philippe, tried to follow him for a time.

Backstage, Raoul was stopped by the group of ballet girls standing outside the dressing rooms. But at last he was able to slip past them.

The Count Turned to Raoul.

In Christine's dressing room, Raoul saw that the theater doctor had just arrived. Christine lay on a sofa, her eyes closed, in the midst of a room full of people.

Raoul bent close to her, then asked, "Don't you think, Doctor, that everyone should leave? There's no air to breathe in here."

"You're right," said the doctor. He sent everyone but Raoul away.

Raoul stayed and watched Christine as her eyes opened. She turned her head. When she saw Raoul, she sat up, her eyes wide with surprise. She looked at the doctor, and then at Raoul again, and asked in a whisper, "Who are you?"

"Miss Daaé," Raoul said, gazing into her eyes. "Don't you know me? I am the little boy who went into the sea to retrieve your scarf."

She stared at him and gave a little laugh, as if he must be making a joke about knowing her.

Raoul turned red at the thought that she

"It is the ghost! The Opera Phantom!" one girl cried again to the other dancers. Silence fell in the dressing room. Then the girl, with terror on her face, whispered, "Listen!"

They seemed to hear a rustling outside the dressing-room door. There was no sound of footsteps. The rustling was like light silk brushing over the panel.

Then it stopped.

Madam Sorelli tried to show more courage than the others. She went to the door and asked, "Who's there?"

But nobody answered.

Feeling all eyes upon her, she made an effort not to show her fear, and said loudly, "Is there anyone behind the door?"

"Oh, yes, yes! Of course there is!" cried a girl named Meg, holding Madam Sorelli back by her skirt. "Whatever you do, don't open the door!"

But Madam Sorelli opened the door. The girls ran to the other side of the dressing room.

Madam Sorelli looked into the hall. It was

She Slammed the Door Closed.

empty. Only a gas lamp flickered warmly in the empty passage.

The chief dancer slammed the door closed. "No," she said, "there is no one there."

"Still, we saw him!" one girl said, coming back to stand beside Madam Sorelli. "He must be somewhere. We had better all go downstairs together to hear the managers' speech and then we will come up again together."

"Come, pull yourselves together! No one has ever really seen the ghost," Madam Sorelli said to the girls.

"Yes, yes, we saw him—we saw him just now!" cried the girls. "He had a death's head and black clothes!"

No one said anything for a moment. Then Meg said, "Hush! Mother says the ghost doesn't like being talked about."

"And why does your mother say so?" someone asked.

"Because...because...nothing...I swore not

to tell!" Meg stammered.

The other girls kept at her and promised they would keep the secret, too, until Meg, with her eyes fixed on the door, said, "Well, it's because of the private box."

"What private box?"

"The Phantom's box!" Meg said.

"Has the ghost a private opera box? Oh, do tell us!" another dancer chimed in.

"Not so loud!" Meg said. "It's Box Five. You know, the box on the grand balcony, on the left. That's the ghost's box."

"And does the Phantom really come there?" asked one girl, shivering.

"Yes. The ghost comes, but only when there is nobody there. You can only hear him when he is in his theater box. But we should not talk of these things. It will bring bad luck," Meg said.

Madam Sorelli turned pale. "I shall never be able to give my speech to the managers before

"The Phantom's Box!" Meg Said.

they leave tonight," she complained.

She left her dressing room to go downstairs to the farewell party being given for the managers. The ballet girls followed right behind her, staying close to her and each other, clinging together as they crept fearfully downstairs and through the dark hall.

CHAPTER 2

The New Opera Star

Downstairs, Madam Sorelli met a nobleman she knew, Count Philippe. The count was very excited. "Madam Sorelli, what an evening! And Christine Daaé—how magnificently she sang tonight!" he said.

"Impossible!" said one of the dancers. "Six months ago, she squawked like a crow!" But that night at the Opera had been special. No other performance had been quite like it. All the great composers had led the orchestra in playing their greatest works.

The Audience Went Mad with Delight.

Christine Daaé, for the first time ever, had sung like an angel.

She had begun with a song from *Romeo and Juliet*. It was the first time anyone had sung that music at the Opera. And when the famous singer Madam Carlotta suddenly became ill, Christine sang the last part of the opera *Faust* in Madam Carlotta's place.

The whole audience went mad with delight, rising to its feet, shouting, cheering, and clapping. Overcome by this, Christine had fainted in the arms of the other singers and was quickly carried off the stage.

Count Philippe had applauded for Christine, too. He was from a proud, old noble family. He had two sisters and a brother named Raoul. The two sisters were married, but the count still watched after his younger brother, who was just twenty-one.

The count was proud of Raoul and arranged for him to be in the Navy, perhaps even one day becoming an admiral.

Just now, with Raoul on leave from the Navy, the count planned to show Raoul around Paris and tonight had brought Raoul to the Opera.

That evening, the count, after applauding for Christine, turned to Raoul and saw that he had turned pale. "What's the matter?" he asked.

Raoul just stood there. Then he said, "Let's go and meet Miss Daaé. She has never sung like that before."

They left their seats and made their way to the door that led to the stage. At the stage, they pushed through the crowd with Raoul leading the way.

Raoul felt that his heart was no longer even in his chest. He felt hollow. His brother, Count Philippe, tried to follow him for a time.

Backstage, Raoul was stopped by the group of ballet girls standing outside the dressing rooms. But at last he was able to slip past them.

The Count Turned to Raoul.

In Christine's dressing room, Raoul saw that the theater doctor had just arrived. Christine lay on a sofa, her eyes closed, in the midst of a room full of people.

Raoul bent close to her, then asked, "Don't you think, Doctor, that everyone should leave? There's no air to breathe in here."

"You're right," said the doctor. He sent everyone but Raoul away.

Raoul stayed and watched Christine as her eyes opened. She turned her head. When she saw Raoul, she sat up, her eyes wide with surprise. She looked at the doctor, and then at Raoul again, and asked in a whisper, "Who are you?"

"Miss Daaé," Raoul said, gazing into her eyes. "Don't you know me? I am the little boy who went into the sea to retrieve your scarf."

She stared at him and gave a little laugh, as if he must be making a joke about knowing her.

Raoul turned red at the thought that she

would laugh at him. He stood up. "You are pretending not to remember me, but I should like to say something to you, something for only you to hear."

"When I am better, if you please?" she said, her voice shaking.

"Yes, you must go," said the doctor.

"I am not ill now," Christine snapped, with a sudden burst of temper. She stood up and brushed her hand over her eyes. "Thank you, Doctor. I should like to be alone now! Please go away, all of you. Leave me."

The doctor shook his head unhappily, but he went out, taking Raoul with him. Outside Christine's dressing room, he said to Raoul, "She does not seem herself tonight." Then he said goodnight and Raoul was left alone.

That part of the Opera House was empty now. The good-bye party for the managers was taking place up at the front of the Opera House near the grand entrance. Raoul thought that Christine

But Then He Heard a Man's Voice.

might go to the party, and so he waited in the silence and the shadows for her.

One idea alone filled his burning brain. Christine must have wanted to be left alone for his sake! After all, he had told her that he wanted to speak to her without others around.

He went back to her room and, with his ear to the door to hear her answer, he started to knock.

But then he heard a man's voice, low and odd. "Christine, you must love me!" said the voice.

"How can you doubt my love, when I sing only for you!" Christine answered, her voice sad and trembling.

Raoul leaned against the door to ease his pain. Christine loved someone else!

The man's voice spoke again. "Are you very tired?" the man asked.

"Oh, tonight I gave you my soul and I am dead!" Christine said.

Raoul had to keep himself from bursting in.

"Your soul is a beautiful thing, child," the voice said. "And I thank you. No king ever had so good a gift. The angels wept tonight."

Raoul knew he should go away. He should not be caught listening at a door. He stepped away and waited in a dark corner for the man to leave the room.

Raoul learned what love meant that night, and hatred. He wanted to know the face of this man he now hated.

Suddenly, the door opened. Christine came out, her face hidden behind a lace veil. She was alone. She closed the door behind her, but she did not lock it. She hurried past Raoul. He did not follow her but waited for the man he had heard speaking in Christine's dressing room.

When the hall was empty again, Raoul went to Christine's room, opened the door, went in, and shut the door behind him. He found himself in darkness. The gaslight had been put out.

"There is someone here!" he said, with his

Christine Hurried Past Raoul.

back against the closed door. "Why are you hiding?"

All was darkness and silence. Raoul heard only the sound of his own breathing. "If you don't answer, you are a coward! But I'll still see you!" he said.

He struck a match. The blaze lit up the dressing room. The room was empty!

CHAPTER 3

The Mysterious Reason

With his match, Raoul lit the gaslights again. Then he opened the cupboards and closets and felt the walls with his hands. Nothing!

"Am I going mad?" he asked himself.

Raoul stood for ten minutes, with only the sound of the gas lamps hissing softly in the silence of the empty room. Then he left, bewildered by the mystery.

He tried to find Christine after that. He went to the party for the managers. Everyone seemed to be laughing and having a good time.

She Could Not Give Her Speech.

Then Madam Sorelli stepped forward to give her speech. As she did, a girl screamed.

"The Phantom of the Opera!" a man shouted.

Everyone turned, and it seemed to Raoul that he saw a shadow and red eyes, but then the figure vanished.

Two men stepped forward to calm the dancer who had screamed. But Madam Sorelli could not give her speech now. The old managers each kissed her, and then they gave the keys to the Opera House to the new managers. There were two master keys that opened the thousands of doors at the Opera House.

"Never sell the Opera ghost's box," Monsieur Poligny, one of the old managers, warned the new managers.

The two new managers looked at each other and smiled, as if this must be some joke.

Raoul turned away from them. But he could not find Christine.

The next day, and the day after that, Raoul

tried to meet Christine. But she would not see him, not even when he followed her. She seemed to see nobody. Raoul suffered, for he was shy and she was very beautiful. He dared not talk about his love, not even to himself. But her angel's voice had captured his heart.

He wondered constantly who the man was who had been behind the door saying, "You must love me!" Why had there been no one in the room when he looked? And why had Christine not recognized him?

Finally, Raoul wrote to her. She sent him back a note that said:

I have not forgotten the little boy who went into the sea to retrieve my scarf. I feel that I must write to you today. I am going to Perros. Tomorrow is the anniversary of the death of my poor father. He is buried in Perros with his violin, in the graveyard of the little church.

Christine's father had been a great

Finally, Raoul Wrote to Her.

musician, Raoul knew. When Christine was six, her mother had died and her father had begun to travel in search of fame and fortune. Christine's father, however, had found nothing but poverty. But Christine had loved him.

Raoul dressed as quickly as he could, wrote a note to his brother and took a carriage to the train station to follow Christine. He read Christine's note over and over again, and remembered how they had first met in Perros when they were children.

Raoul had been in Perros with his family. One day, he had seen a little girl at the seashore cry out when the wind took her scarf into the sea.

"It's all right! I'll get your scarf out of the sea," Raoul had told her. He had gotten himself very wet, but he had reached the scarf and Christine had laughed and kissed him. That had been the start of their spending time together, even though Raoul was from an old, rich family and Christine from a poor one.

When the train stopped, Raoul took a carriage to the small town of Perros. He questioned the carriage driver and learned that a young lady who looked like a Parisian had also traveled to Perros. She had gone to the inn known as the Setting Sun.

When Raoul walked into the smoky front room of the Setting Sun, he saw Christine standing there. She was smiling, and showed no surprise at seeing him.

"So you have come," she said. "I felt that I would find you here when I came back from the church. Someone told me that I would see you."

"Who?" asked Raoul, taking her hand in his.

"Why, my poor father, who is dead," Christine said.

Raoul looked at her in surprise. "Did your father tell you that I love you, Christine? And that I cannot live without you?"

Her cheeks red, Christine turned her head

"I Thought You Would Remember."

away. "Me? You are dreaming, my old friend," she said, her voice trembling. And then she laughed.

"Don't laugh, Christine!" Raoul pleaded.

She shook her head. "I did not make you come here to tell me such things as that."

"But you knew that your letter would make me follow you to Perros. How can you not have thought I loved you?"

"I thought you would remember our time here when we were children. Perhaps I was wrong to write to you. But when I saw you again, it reminded me of the past and made me write to you as if I were still the little girl I was then."

Raoul looked at her and saw both fear and warmth for him in her eyes. But what did she fear? And was there more than a friend's love there, in her eyes?

"But why, when you saw me in your room and I reminded you that I had rescued your scarf from the sea, why did you answer as though you did not know me?" he asked.

She stared at Raoul without saying a word. "You don't answer me!" he said, angry and unhappy. "Well, I will answer for you. It was because there was someone in that room that night, and you did not want him to know we had once been friends!"

"Who are you talking about?" Christine asked.

"The man to whom you said, 'I sing only for you! Tonight I gave you my soul and I am dead!'"

Christine seized Raoul's arm and clutched it. "Then you were listening behind the door? What else did you hear?" she asked, becoming strangely calm and letting go of Raoul's arm.

"I heard him say to you, 'Christine, you must love me!'" Raoul answered.

At these words, a deathly pallor spread over Christine's face. Dark shadows seemed to form around her eyes. She staggered and seemed about to faint. Raoul darted forward with his arms out, but Christine pushed him back.

Christine Seized Raoul's Arm.

"Go on! Go on! Tell me all you heard!" she said in a low voice.

Raoul told her everything he had heard that night outside her dressing room.

Christine put her hand to her heart. Then two tears dropped, like two pearls, down her pale cheeks.

"Christine!" Raoul said, trying to take her in his arms. But she ran away from him, her hair loose and flying, and locked herself in her room.

Raoul did not know what to do. He waited, hoping Christine would come back. With nothing else to do, he walked to the church graveyard. Red roses had blossomed in the morning, in the snow—life among the dead.

He said a prayer for Christine, and then he climbed a hill and sat down on the edge to look at the sea. The wind fell with the evening. Raoul was surrounded by icy darkness, but he did not feel the cold. It was here, he remembered, as he sat alone and shivering in the dark, that he used to come with little Christine to watch the moon rise.

He smiled at the thought. Then a voice behind him said, "Do you think we will see the moon rise this evening?"

It was Christine. He tried to speak, but she put her gloved hand to his mouth.

"Listen, Raoul. I have decided to tell you something serious, very serious. Do you remember the legend of the Angel of Music?"

"I do," he said. "I believe it was here that your father first told that story to us."

"And it was here that he said, 'When I am in heaven, my child, I will send him to you.' Well, Raoul, my father is in heaven, and I have been visited by the Angel of Music."

"I have no doubt of it," said Raoul, for it seemed to him that she must be thinking of her father and remembering how incredibly she had sung at the Opera for the big gala.

"How do you understand all of this?" she

"You Have Heard the Angel of Music."

asked, bringing her pale face close to his.

"I understand," he said, "that no one can sing as you did the other evening without some miracle. You have heard the Angel of Music, Christine."

"Yes. In my dressing room. That is where he comes to give me my lessons daily. And I have not been the only one to hear him," she said.

"Who else has heard him, Christine?"

"You, my friend. The other evening, it was he who was talking to me when you were listening behind the door. It was he who said, 'You must love me.'"

Raoul burst out laughing. The first light of the moon appeared and cast its soft beams on them. Christine turned on Raoul. Her eyes, usually so gentle, flashed fire.

"What are you laughing at?" she demanded. "You think you heard just any man's voice?"

"Well..." Raoul started to say. He was not certain what to tell Christine, for everything he said seemed to make her angry.

"What are you thinking?" she asked him. "I am a good girl. I wouldn't be in my dressing room with a man. If you had opened the door, you would have seen there was nobody in the room!"

"That's true! I did open the door after you were gone, and I found no one in the room. But, Christine, I think that somebody is playing a game with you."

She cried out, and ran away. He ran after her.

"Leave me! Leave me!" she called out to him, her tone fierce. And she disappeared.

Raoul returned to the inn feeling tired and sad. He was told that Christine had gone to her bedroom and that she would not be down to dinner. Raoul dined alone. Then he went to his room and tried to read, went to bed and tried to sleep.

He thought again about how he and Christine had first met, and about the time they had spent together in this very town, spent

She Ran Away.

playing together as children. Christine's father had given Raoul violin lessons. In this way, Raoul had learned to love the same songs that Christine loved.

But most of all, Christine loved to hear the story of the Angel of Music from her father. He had said that every great musician, every great artist, received a visit from the Angel at least once in his or her life. No one ever saw the Angel, but he was heard by those meant to hear him.

Had Christine really heard the Angel of Music? Raoul wondered.

Then he heard someone moving around in the room next to his. It must be Christine, he thought. She had not gone to bed.

He heard Christine's door open and then close. Where could she be going? It was almost midnight. Opening his own door, Raoul saw Christine slipping along the hallway. She went down the stairs. He followed her as she walked out of the inn.

Christine seemed not to hear Raoul's steps. She acted as if he were not even there. She walked up the road. The church clock struck a quarter to twelve. Raoul thought that this made her hurry, for she began almost to run toward the church.

The moonlight on the snow made the night nearly as bright as day.

In the churchyard, tombstones lay partly hidden under the snow. Raoul had never seen a night so clear—or so cold.

Raoul had been worried. Now he knew that Christine was headed to her father's grave again, for she now knelt beside it. At that moment, it struck midnight.

And then Raoul heard the most perfectly beautiful music. Raoul remembered what Christine had said about the Angel of Music.

The song playing was *The Resurrection of Lazarus*. When the music stopped, Raoul heard a noise. It came from the heap of bones that made

Raoul Saw a Terrible Death's Head.

up a wall near the church. It was as if they were chuckling, and Raoul could not help shuddering.

Then Christine stood up and walked slowly to the gate. She seemed lost in the music.

Before Raoul could go to her, a skull rolled from the wall of skeletons. Then another rolled at him. Then another. He stared at them.

And then Raoul saw a shadow glide along the wall of skulls. The shadow went into the church and Raoul followed. Inside the church, he caught hold of the edge of someone's coat.

Moonlight lit Raoul and the shadow through the stained-glass windows of the church.

The shadow turned around. Raoul saw a terrible death's head, with a pair of scorching eyes. Raoul's courage failed. He inhaled sharply, and then sank to the floor.

When Raoul woke the next morning, he found himself at the inn. Someone had found him in the church and had taken him back to his room.

But Christine had gone. She had returned to Paris, leaving him a note that read:

You must have the courage not to see me again, not to speak of me again. If you love me just a little, do this for me. My life depends upon it. Your life depends upon it. Your little Christine.

". . .Do This for Me."

CHAPTER 4

The Fatal Performance

Christine was back in Paris. After the gala night at the opera, she behaved as if she could not control her future, and as if she feared success.

She knew that Count Philippe, to please his brother Raoul, had worked to help her singing career with the Paris Opera House. She wrote to thank the count and also to ask him to stop speaking in her favor. Christine was frightened.

"I don't know myself when I sing," she wrote to him. But she knew she must sing again.

On the next Saturday, Madam Carlotta, the star of the Opera, rang for her maid, who brought Madam Carlotta's letters to her in bed. Among them was one written in red ink, which read:

If you appear tonight, you must be prepared for a great misfortune when you sing... a misfortune worse than death.

The letter took away Carlotta's appetite. She sat up in bed and thought hard. It was not the first letter like this she'd had. Other people were jealous of her fame. But she had never had a letter with such threats.

Carlotta also hated that Christine had so many now who loved her singing. She tried to get her friends to tell the Opera House managers not to let Christine sing again. And Carlotta told lies about Christine.

When Carlotta stopped thinking about the rivalry between Christine and herself, her mind turned immediately to the threat in the strange

Madam Carlotta's Friends Were There.

letter she had gotten. The letter must be from Christine, she decided.

We shall see, she said to herself.

She went to her friends and told them about the letter and said that Christine must have written it. She said they must fill the Opera House with Carlotta's own admirers who would not applaud at all for Christine's singing.

At five o'clock a second letter came. It was short and said:

If you are wise, you will see that it is madness to try to sing tonight.

Carlotta sneered, shrugged her shoulders and sang two or three notes to give herself courage.

Madam Carlotta's friends were all at the Paris Opera that night, but they could not see if any of Christine's friends were there to make trouble for Carlotta.

The first act of the opera passed without anything of an unusual nature happening.

Then Christine came onstage. Still nothing happened.

The Opera House managers decided all would be well. Then they went to Box Five—the phantom's box.

The first thing they saw there was a tin of candy sitting on the ledge of the private box. Who had put it there? They asked the box keepers, but none of them knew. The two managers looked at each other. Then they felt a curious sort of chilly draft around them. They sat down in silence to watch the rest of the opera from the box seats.

Christine came onstage to sing the part of Margarita. As she sang her first two lines with a bunch of roses and lilacs in her hand, she looked up and saw Raoul. From that moment, her voice seemed less sure, less crystal-clear than usual. Something seemed to deaden and dull her singing.

"What an odd girl she is!" said one of

A Tin of Candy on the Ledge

Madam Carlotta's friends. "The other night she sang like an angel, and tonight she's simply bleating. As if she has had no lessons."

Raoul, as he listened, thought only of the new letter he had from Christine. She had asked him never to see her again. He put his head into his hands and wept.

Count Philippe, behind Raoul, frowned in anger. He had seen his brother on his return to Paris, pale and looking ill. When Raoul told him about seeing Christine, the count had written to her and asked to see her. She had replied that she could see neither him nor his brother. That had made the count angry, for no one ever refused to see him!

"The little ingrate!" growled the count under his breath. What did this Christine want from his brother? What was she hoping for?

Christine as Margarita finished singing. The audience cheered for her.

Then Madam Carlotta made her entrance onto the stage.

Certain of herself, of her friends in the audience, Carlotta flung herself into her part. She was well applauded. Then a terrible thing happened.

Madam Carlotta opened her mouth to sing again, and instead she croaked like a frog!

Everyone gasped. The Opera House managers, still sitting up in Box Five, stared in horror. It had to be evil magic. How could this happen? The managers shivered and felt their hair stand on end. The Phantom was there—around them, behind them, beside them, they were sure.

They felt him there without seeing him; they heard his breath. They trembled. They thought of running away, but dared not move or say anything that would let the ghost know that they knew he was there!

What was going to happen next?

Bravely, Carlotta started to sing again.

The Chandelier Came Smashing Down.

But all that came out of her mouth was another frog-like croak.

The audience broke out in unhappy yells. The Opera House managers sat in their chairs and dared not even turn around. Behind them, they heard the ghost chuckling. Then they heard his voice.

"She is singing tonight to bring the chandelier down!" the unseen voice boomed.

Hearing a noise of rattling crystal, the managers looked up to the painted ceiling of the Opera House and uttered terrible cries. The enormous crystal chandelier was slipping down at the call of the Phantom's voice. Released from its hook, the great chandelier plunged from the ceiling and came smashing into the middle of the Opera House theater, amid a thousand shouts of terror and a wild rush for the doors.

CHAPTER 5

Christine Is Gone

The Paris newspapers reported the next day that many people had been hurt in the accident at the Opera House. Madam Carlotta fell ill. And Christine disappeared. For the next two weeks, no one saw her at the Opera or anywhere else in Paris.

Raoul was the first to notice that Christine had vanished. Despite Christine's letter asking him not to speak to her, he wrote to her. But she did not answer. And he did not see her name listed to sing at the Opera House.

The Newspapers Reported the Accident.

One afternoon he went to the managers' office to ask where Christine had gone. He found them both looking worried.

The police had said that chandelier's fall had been an accident. The chains had worn out. But the managers could not help thinking they should have found out about that before it happened. They blamed themselves that they had not fixed the chains before so many people were hurt.

When Raoul came to ask about Christine, he was told she was taking a holiday, for reasons of health.

"Then she is ill! What is the matter with her?" he cried.

"We don't know," one manager answered.

Raoul remembered Christine's letter, which told him not to try to see her. But the voice he had heard in her room troubled him. What if someone was playing an evil trick on her? He thought of one person who might be able to help him,

Madam Valérius.

Madam Valérius had known Christine for years and had helped Christine after her father had died. Raoul knew that Madam Valérius now lived in Paris, and so he went to see her.

As Raoul stepped into the room where Madam Valérius lived, he saw that her hair had turned white, yet her eyes still looked bright as a child's.

"Raoul!" she cried happily, putting out both her hands to him. "Ah, it's heaven that sends you here!"

"Madame, where is Christine?" he asked eagerly.

"She is with her good genius," the old lady replied calmly. "The Angel of Music. You must not tell anybody." She put her finger to her lips, to warn him to be silent.

"You can rely on me," said Raoul.

"I know! I know I can. I am very fond of you, Raoul, you know. And so is Christine!"

"He Forbids Her To!"

"What makes you think that Christine is fond of me, madame?" he asked in a low voice.

"She used to speak of you every day. But did you think that Christine was free?"

"What! Is Christine engaged to be married?" Raoul asked, in a choking voice.

"Why, no! Christine couldn't marry, even if she wanted to! Because of the Angel of Music, of course! He forbids her to!"

"The Angel of Music forbids her to marry?" Raoul echoed in disbelief.

"She told me that the Angel said if she got married, she would never hear him again. You understand that she can't let the Angel of Music go. I thought Christine told you all this, when she met you at Perros. The Angel of Music met her there in the churchyard, at her father's grave."

"Madame, you will have the goodness to tell me where that genius lives," Raoul said, angry now that Christine had not told him this.

"In heaven," the old lady said.

He did not know what to say to her. How could the Angel of Music come down from heaven to haunt the Paris Opera? Was Madam Valérius also being tricked?

"How long has she known this angel?" Raoul demanded.

"It's about three months since he began to give her lessons."

"And where does he give her these lessons?" Raoul asked, unable to understand any of this.

"Now that she has gone away with him, I can't say. But he used to teach Christine in her dressing room."

"I see!" said Raoul. Then he said good-bye to Madam Valérius.

Raoul walked home to his brother's house in a pitiful state. He could have struck himself, banged his head against the walls! He had believed Christine when she had talked about the Angel of Music! But now he thought that her

Raoul Walked Home in a Pitiful State.

"angel" must be some other attractive singer. Raoul felt sure now that he had been silly to think anyone was tricking Christine.

His brother was waiting for him, but Raoul could not tell him about the Angel of Music. It seemed too silly.

Raoul's brother asked him to come out to dinner. Raoul started to say no–but then the count said that Christine had been seen in Paris the night before. She had been in a carriage. The friend with her was only a shadowy outline in the dark. The carriage had driven at a slow pace along a lonely lane near the Paris racetrack.

That night was very cold. The road seemed empty, brightly lit by moonlight. Raoul took a carriage to the racetrack. He told the driver to wait for him at the corner of the road that ran behind the racetrack. Then Raoul hid himself at the roadside. He hugged himself against the cold, stamping his feet to keep warm.

Half an hour later a carriage turned the corner of the road and came toward him. The horse pulling the carriage moved at a walking pace. As the big black carriage came near, Raoul saw a woman inside. The moonlight shone pale on her face.

"Christine!" Raoul called. Then he realized that he should not have spoken out loud. Once he said her name, the carriage window closed. The driver whipped the horses into a run. The carriage sped past Raoul.

Raoul ran after it.

"Christine!" he called out again. But it was no use. He stopped, peering down the cold road into the darkness. Nothing was colder than his heart at that moment— nothing half so dead!

He had seen her with someone else in that carriage. The shadow of a man. And she had passed him by without answering him. He wanted to die.

Raoul went home and spent the rest of the

The Letter Was Covered with Mud.

night sitting on his bed. But the next morning brought him a surprise letter.

The letter was covered with mud, and unstamped. On it was written, "To be handed to Raoul de Chagny," with the address in pencil. It must have been flung out into the street in the hope that someone walking past would pick it up and deliver it.

As soon as Raoul saw the writing, he knew it was Christine's. He opened the letter and read:

Dear, go to the masked ball at the Opera on the night after tomorrow. At twelve o'clock, be in the little room behind the big meeting-room. Don't mention this to anyone. Wear a white cape and a mask. As you love me, do not let yourself be seen. Christine.

CHAPTER 6

At the Masked Ball

Raoul read the letter again and again. Why did Christine now write to him? And just what had she been dragged into? What monster had carried her off and by what means? He asked himself these questions over and over.

Or was she playing a cruel game with him? Was she out to make him look like a fool?

He no longer knew whether to pity Christine or to curse her.

However, two nights later, with a mask on his face and wearing a white cape, Raoul went to

Wearing a White Cape

the Opera House. He felt foolish. However, he was sure that no one would ever recognize him.

The ball at the Opera House was expected to be much more crowded than any other masked ball. By midnight, it seemed as if every artist in Paris was there. Everyone was dressed in costumes and masks. Some wore long old-fashioned clothes.

Raoul climbed the grand staircase in the Opera House at five minutes to twelve. Crossing the big meeting-room, he entered the smaller room mentioned in Christine's letter. He found the room crowded, with people going back and forth from the next room to get their suppers and returning with their food.

Raoul leaned against a doorway and waited. He did not have to wait long. A masked figure in a black cape passed. A pale hand reached out from beneath the cape and quickly squeezed Raoul's hand.

"Is that you, Christine?" Raoul whispered.

The black-caped figure turned around and the woman in the cape raised her finger to her lips. No doubt it was to warn him not to mention her name again. Raoul followed her in silence.

He was afraid of losing her. He was ready now to forgive her for anything. No doubt, she would soon tell him why she had acted so strangely toward him.

As Raoul once more passed through the great meeting-room, he saw a group crowded around a man dressed in scarlet. He wore a huge hat and feathers on top of a death's head mask. From the man's shoulders hung an immense red-velvet cape. Gold letters on it read, "Don't touch me! I am Red Death stalking abroad!"

Raoul almost forgot about Christine, so much did the man in red startle him. But the black-caped figure caught him by the arm and dragged him from the room where Red Death stalked.

She hurried Raoul forward as though they

"Stay at the Back," She Warned Him.

were being chased. Raoul thought he glimpsed a figure in red following them. They ran up two flights. Christine led Raoul into a private box.

"Stay at the back of the box," she warned him in a whisper.

Christine moved to the back of the box and listened at the door. She must be afraid that someone had followed them, Raoul knew.

"Ah, he must have gone up the stairs to a higher floor," Christine said, and stepped away from the door.

"Who? Who do you mean?" Raoul said, taking off his mask. Christine kept hers on.

"Can't you tell me what all this means?" Raoul cried. "What have you been doing these past two weeks? What is this tale about the Angel of Music, which you have told me and Madam Valérius? Explain yourself, Christine! What is this farce?"

"Dear Raoul, it is a tragedy!" Christine

said, and she took off her mask.

Raoul saw her face and let out a cry of surprise. A deathly pallor had robbed her skin of color, and sorrow had added lines and shadows under her eyes.

"My dearest! Forgive me," he said, holding out his arms, unable to bear how ill she looked.

"This must be good-bye, Raoul," Christine said, her voice sad. "You shall not see me again. I came to tell you why, but I can't tell you now... you would not believe me! You have lost faith in me, Raoul. We are finished!"

She put on her mask again and left, stopping him with a gesture so he would not follow her.

He watched her until she was out of sight. Then he also went down among the crowd, hardly knowing what he was doing. The man in red had followed them, he knew. Was that man Christine's Angel of Music?

Raoul began to search the rooms for the man

"You Have Lost Faith in Me."

in red. He asked everyone if they had seen the Red Death. But he could find no one who knew any man who wore such a costume.

At two in the morning, Raoul walked down the passage that led to Christine's dressing room.

He knocked at the door. There was no answer. He entered, as he had when he had looked for "the man's voice." The room was empty. A gas lamp was burning, turned down low. Then he heard steps in the passage. He had only just enough time to hide behind a curtain.

Christine came into the room, took off her mask and flung it on the table. She sighed and let her head fall into her hands.

"Poor Erik!" she muttered.

Raoul frowned. What had this Erik to do with Christine? Was Erik the man in red? And why did she not say "Poor Raoul" now, after what had happened between them?

Christine began to write a note. Writing

fast, she filled four sheets of paper. Suddenly, she raised her head and hid the papers in her pocket. She seemed to be listening. Raoul also listened.

He heard a strange sound, a faint singing that seemed to come from the walls. A very beautiful, soft voice came nearer and nearer through the walls; a man's voice.

"Here I am, Erik," Christine said, rising. "I am ready. But you are late."

Raoul peered out from behind the curtain. He saw only Christine's face. She smiled the way a sick person might, with her first hope of getting better.

The voice without a body went on singing. Raoul had never in his life heard anything so sweet or so powerful. He now began to understand how Christine could sing like an angel after hearing this voice.

The voice was singing the wedding-night song from the opera *Romeo and Juliet*. Raoul saw

He Had to Break Her Free from the Spell.

Christine stretch out her arms to the voice.

"Fate links thee to me forever and a day!" the voice sang.

The music went straight through Raoul's heart. He knew he had to break Christine free from the spell of that voice. Raoul pulled back the curtain that had hidden him and stepped into the dressing room.

Christine was standing with her back to him. She faced the far side of the room where there was a mirror as large as the wall. The mirror reflected her image, but not that of Raoul, for he was just behind her and hidden by her reflection.

Christine walked toward her image in the mirror, her image moving closer to her. The "two Christines" touched—the real one touching the reflected Christine.

"Fate links thee to me forever and a day!" sang the voice again.

Raoul reached for Christine, but he was

suddenly flung back. An icy blast swept over his face. He saw two, then four, then eight, then twenty Christines spinning around him. They moved so fast he could not touch one of them. At last, everything stood still again. Raoul could see himself in the mirror—but Christine had disappeared.

Which way had she gone? From which way would she return—or would she ever return at all?

Eight Christines!

CHAPTER 7

A Terrible Secret

Raoul rushed up to the mirror. He struck at his reflection. The room still echoed with that distant singing. Where had Christine gone? Is this what she had meant when she had said good-bye to him? Worn out, feeling defeated, Raoul sat down on a small chair. His head fell into his hands. Tears filled his eyes. He loved Christine. And now she had left him... for someone else, it seemed.

"Who is this Erik?" Raoul wondered aloud.

The next day Raoul went back to visit Madam Valérius. When he arrived, he gasped. To his surprise, there was Christine herself— seated by the bedside of the old lady.

The lovely pink and white color had come back to Christine's cheeks. The dark shadows that had dulled her eyes were gone. Raoul no longer saw the pitiful face he had seen the day before.

Christine rose without any showing of feeling. She gave Raoul her hand. Raoul's shock was so great that he stood motionless, unable to speak.

"Well, Raoul," said Madam Valérius. "Don't you know our Christine? Her good genius has sent her back to us!"

"I thought there was to be no more talk about that!" Christine said. "You know there is no such thing as the Angel of Music!"

"But, child, he gave you lessons for three months. You cannot deny his being with you these months!" Madam

"I Have Promised to Explain Everything."

Valérius insisted.

"I have promised to explain everything to you someday soon. Until then, you are to ask me no more questions!" Christine exclaimed.

"Only if you promised never to leave me again! But you have not promised that," said Madam Valérius.

"All this cannot interest Raoul, anyway," Christine said, glancing at him.

"Not true," said Raoul, in a voice that he tried to make firm, but which was still shaky. "After what happened yesterday, I did not think I would see you here. But why do you keep a secret that may harm you?"

"Is Christine in danger?" cried Madam Valérius.

"Yes, madame," said Raoul.

"Then you must tell me everything, Christine! And what is the danger, Raoul?" The old woman gasped for breath.

"There is a terrible mystery around us,

around Christine. A mystery much more to be feared than any number of ghosts!"

"Don't believe him," Christine said, taking Madam Valérius's hand.

"Then tell me that you will never leave me again," implored the old woman.

"That is a promise I cannot make," said Christine.

"You must let us protect you," Raoul insisted.

"I control my actions, Raoul. You do not. You are not my husband and I will never m arry!" she said, raising up her hands as if to push him away.

Raoul turned pale as he saw the plain gold ring on Christine's finger.

"You have no husband and yet you wear a wedding ring," he said. He tried to take her hand, but she pulled it back.

"That's a present!" Christine said, her cheeks red. She clasped her hands together, as if to hide the ring.

"Yet You Wear a Wedding Ring!"

"Christine! As you have no husband, that ring can only have been given to you by someone who hopes to make you his wife! Why make me feel still worse?" Raoul pleaded.

"Don't you think you have asked me enough questions?" said Christine almost angrily.

"Forgive me, Christine. But I have seen more than you know," Raoul said, shaking his head.

"What did you see, or think you saw?" Christine asked.

"I saw you smile at the sound of the voice that came from the wall, or from the next room to yours. That is what worries me. You are under a spell. And yet today you say there is no Angel of Music! Why, then, did you look as if you were really hearing angels last night?

"It is a very dangerous voice, Christine, for when I heard it, I was myself so captivated by it, you seemed to vanish before my eyes!

"Christine, in the name of heaven, tell us

the name of the man who has put a ring on your finger!"

"Raoul," the girl declared coldly, "you shall never know!"

"And, if she does love that man, Raoul, it is no business of yours!" Madam Valérius said, squeezing Christine's hand.

"I know, madame," Raoul said. "I believe Christine really does love him. But I am not certain that this man has earned her love!"

"It is for me to be the judge of that!" said Christine, looking angrily at Raoul.

Raoul looked back at Christine, darkly. "A man who takes such steps to gain a girl's love..."

"The man must be either a villain, or the girl a fool—is that it?" Christine interrupted. "How can you say that of a man you have never seen?"

"I at least know the name you thought to keep from me. The name of your Angel of Music, is no longer a mystery. I know his name

"Do You Want to Risk Your Life?"

is Erik!"

"Who told you?" Christine could barely whisper, turning white as a sheet.

"You yourself! On the night of the masked ball. When you went to your dressing room and you said, 'Poor Erik.' Well, Christine, there was a poor Raoul who heard you."

"This is the second time you have listened behind the door, Raoul!"

"I was not behind the door. I was in your dressing room!" Raoul said.

"Oh, unhappy man!" moaned the girl, her face pale and her hands trembling. "Unhappy man! Do you want to risk your life?"

"Perhaps," Raoul said, with both love and hopelessness in his voice.

Christine could not keep from weeping. She took his hands and looked at him.

"Raoul," she said tearfully, "forget the man's voice, and do not even remember his name. You must never try to learn the mystery of the man's voice."

"Is the mystery so very terrible?" Raoul asked.

"There is no more awful mystery. Swear to me that you will make no attempt to find out," she begged. "Swear to me that you will never come to my dressing room, unless I send for you."

"Then you promise to send for me before long, Christine?"

"I promise," Christine vowed, nodding.

"When?" Raoul asked.

"Tomorrow," she told him.

"Then I swear to do as you ask," Raoul said.

He kissed her hands and went away, cursing Erik, telling himself he must wait for Christine to trust him enough to be able to tell him everything. But how was he to wait, when every time he saw her, she left him more and more bewildered by her changing moods?

He Kissed Her Hands.

CHAPTER 8

Trapdoors

The next day, Raoul saw Christine at the Opera House. She still wore the plain gold ring. But she was kind to him. She talked to him about his future. He had received word that in a month he was to sail with the Navy on a voyage to the North Pole.

"Then in a month we shall have to say good-bye," she said.

"Not if we promise to wait for each other forever," he told her.

"Hush, Raoul!" she said, putting her hand

to his mouth. "You know we shall never be married. We cannot. That is understood! But we can pretend. We can pretend that we will be. In a month, you will go away—but I can be happy for the rest of my life that first we will have had this one month together."

Raoul bowed to Christine. "May I have the honor to ask for your hand?" he said, as if he really were asking for her to marry him.

"Why, you have both of them already," she told him. She smiled at him for the first time in a long while. Raoul suddenly felt already as happy as he could hope to be.

They began to spend as much time together as they could. Christine took Raoul throughout the giant Opera House; she showed him its dressing rooms and stairs and its great stage, and all the rooms that held scenery, costumes, and all the other things people used on the stage of an enormous theater.

Since the night that Madam Carlotta had

Christine Got Thunderous Applause.

sung like a frog, she had not been able to sing again. Now the managers had begun to give Christine all the parts that Madam Charlotta could not sing. Christine got thunderous applause every time she appeared.

Raoul watched her success. But he saw that Christine still wore the plain gold ring which someone else had given her. He did not like that, for it made him very jealous.

Christine also seemed frightened. Raoul asked her why. "I swear—it is nothing," she answered. "Nothing."

But once, when they walked past an open trapdoor on the stage, Raoul stopped.

"You have shown me all over the upper part of the Opera House, Christine, but I have heard strange stories told of the lower part. Shall we go down there?"

She caught him by the arm, as if she feared to see him go down the black hole left by the open trapdoor. "I will not have you go there!

Everything that is underground belongs to him!" she whispered, her voice trembling.

"So he lives down there, does he?" Raoul said, his voice rough. He knew she must be talking about Erik.

"I never said so. Come away! Come!" she said, desperately tugging him from the spot.

"I will remove you from his power, Christine, I swear it," Raoul said. "You won't have to think of him anymore."

"Is it possible?" she asked. "He has followed me away from Paris before. Where could I go to escape him?"

"I shall hide you in some unknown corner of the world, where he cannot come to look for you. You will be safe. Then I will go away, as you have sworn never to marry."

Christine took Raoul's hands. Suddenly, she heard a noise. She turned her head to look. Then she dragged Raoul up the stairs.

"Higher!" was all she said, her eyes wide

"Everything Underground Belongs to Him!"

with fear. "Higher still!"

She looked behind her as if watching for a shadow that followed.

Finally they reached the roof. Christine ran to the open space between the three domes of the Opera House. On the middle dome, at the very highest point of the Opera House, stood a statue of the Greek god Apollo.

Below, all of Paris lay before them, like a magical valley of buildings and twinkling lights. It was a spring evening. Clouds glowing gold and purple from the setting sun drifted by.

Christine sat down near the huge middle dome under the statue of Apollo. "If the moment comes for you to take me away and I refuse to go with you—you must carry me off by force!" she told Raoul.

"Are you afraid you will change your mind, Christine?" Raoul asked, sitting down.

"I don't know," she said, shaking her head. "He is a demon!" She shivered. "I am afraid that he might make me go back to live with him underground!"

"What makes you go back to him, Christine?" Raoul asked.

"If I do not go to him, terrible things may happen! I know I ought to be sorry for him. But he is too horrible! And yet, if I do not go, he will drag me. Again and again, he will tell me he loves me! And he will cry! Oh, those tears, Raoul, those tears in the two black holes where his eyes should be!"

She wrung her hands as Raoul pressed her to his heart. He tried to comfort and reassure her.

"No, no, you shall never again have to hear him tell you he loves you! Let us leave Paris," he said. He tried to rise and lead her away, but she stopped him.

"No," she said, shaking her head sadly. "Let him hear me sing one more time. Tomorrow evening. Then we will go away. I have already promised to sing tomorrow. I must do so. Afterwards, you will come to my dressing room

"Up Here, We Are in No Danger."

at midnight. He will be waiting for me underground. But you shall take me away and we shall be free. You must take me. For if I go back, I fear I shall never return."

She sighed deeply. Then she sat up, a look of fear on her face. "Did you hear something?"

"No," said Raoul, "I heard nothing."

"It is so terrible," she said, "to be always frightened like this! And yet, up here we are in no danger. I have never seen him by daylight. It must be awful! The first time I saw him, I thought he was going to die."

"Tell me how you saw him first," Raoul urged.

"I heard his voice for three months without seeing him. I thought, as you did, that this voice was singing in another room. But I could not find where. And the voice not only sang, but spoke to me and answered my questions. It was as if he understood everything about me. And his voice was beautiful, like the voice of an angel.

It even gave me singing lessons."

Christine stopped for a moment. Then she went on. "I saw you one evening. I was so happy. But the voice was there. It asked about you and so I told the voice about us. Then there was silence. I called to it, but it did not reply. I feared the voice had gone for good, but then I realized it was jealous. And that, dear Raoul, was the moment I knew that I loved you."

Christine stopped and put her head on Raoul's shoulder. They sat quietly like that for some time. They did not see the creeping shadow, a shadow that came along the roof near them.

"The next day," Christine said, "I went back to my dressing room. The voice told me that if I ever gave my heart to someone here on earth, then it must go back to heaven. I did not know if you even loved me. So I swore that you were no more than a brother to me. That was why I refused to see you. I acted as if I didn't remember you. I was so afraid for you. But I

They Did Not See the Creeping Shadow.

could not fool the voice about my feelings!"

"Why did you not at once rid yourself of the voice?" Raoul asked.

"I was not caught until the day I learned the truth! Pity me, Raoul! I want you to know everything!"

"Christine! Something tells me we are wrong to wait. We ought to go at once."

"You are right, Raoul, for certainly he will die when I leave." Then she added in a dull voice, "But we also risk our own lives. He would even commit murder for me."

"But we can find out where he lives. He is not a ghost. We can speak to him and force him to forget you!"

"No, no! There is nothing to be done about Erik except to run away!" Christine said.

"But you were able to run away once," Raoul reminded her.

"But I had to go back to him. You will understand when I tell you everything," she promised.

CHAPTER 9

Christine's Story

Raoul held Christine's hand as if their lives depended on it. She smiled weakly and began to tell him the whole story.

It had been a terrible evening for her, she began. That night, Madam Carlotta had sung like a frog. Then the great chandelier had crashed to the floor, hurting many in the audience. As Christine stood on the stage, she had quivered with fear.

But then that voice she had heard so many times before seemed to command her to come to

A Cold, Bony Hand

it. She followed the voice from the stage to her dressing room. In her room, the mirror that hung on one wall seemed to be growing. She did not know how it happened, but suddenly, she was outside her dressing room in the dark.

She knew she was not dreaming. Afraid, she cried out. A faint red glimmer glowed on a far wall. Suddenly, a cold, bony hand clamped on to her wrist. She cried out again and struggled against it.

The hand dragged her toward the red light. There she saw that she was in the grasp of a man wrapped in a long black coat. He was wearing a mask that hid his face. She opened her mouth to scream, but a hand closed it, a hand that smelled of death.

She fainted.

When she opened her eyes again, she was in darkness. Light from a lantern revealed a bubbling well nearby. The water splashed from the well and onto the place where Christine lay.

Her head rested near the knee of the man in the black coat and mask.

"Who are you?" she asked, trying to push herself away. She wondered in terror if she was the Opera Phantom's prisoner!

She saw then that she lay on the edge of a lake. The waters stretched far into the darkness. A boat was nearby, tied to an iron ring.

She had heard about the legendary lake deep beneath the Opera. The builders had dug far below when they built the huge Opera House—so deep that the very bottom under the bedrock had filled with water, making a lake.

The Phantom put her in the boat and took up a pair of oars. He rowed across the lake. His intense eyes, under the mask, remained fixed on hers.

When the boat reached the other side of the lake, the Phantom got out and again lifted Christine up in his arms. She cried out. Then he hushed her, telling her not to be afraid.

He Rowed Across the Lake.

She fell silent, dazed by a sudden bright light.

The Phantom put her down and she looked around. She was standing in the middle of what seemed a room like any other. The black shape of the man in the mask stood next to her, his arms crossed.

"Don't be afraid, Christine. You are in no danger," said the voice that she knew so well.

Angry now that the Phantom had kidnapped her, she clenched her teeth and lunged at his face. She tried to tear off his mask—to finally see the face behind the voice.

He grabbed at her wrists. "You are in no danger, so long as you do not touch the mask," he said, gently holding her wrists.

He forced Christine to sit in a chair. He went down on his knees in front of her. That gave Christine courage. He could not be a ghost if he could touch her, if he needed chairs and candles and a normal room around him. But who was he, that he lived under the Opera

118

House, so far below the ground?

Frightened, Christine began to cry.

"It is true, Christine! I am not an angel or a ghost. I am Erik!" said the masked man, as if he understood why Christine cried.

"Erik?" she asked.

"I took you away because I love you! I want you to stay with me," Erik said.

Christine stood up. "I can only hate you if you do not give me my freedom."

He stood up too. "You need have no worry. You have no better friend in the world than I. This home is now yours. I will give you everything you need."

She knew then that she had fallen into the hands of a madman. She tried to regain her courage.

"If you are an honest man, then take off your mask," she told him.

"You shall never see Erik's face," he said. She looked away from him. She saw an enormous

"This Is My Work."

organ which filled one whole side of the room. On the desk next to the organ was a music book covered with red notes.

Erik saw her stare at the music book. He let go of her and walked over to it. "This is my work—*Don Juan Triumphant*. I began this twenty years ago. When I have finished it, I shall take it with me into my coffin and never wake up again."

"Will you play me something from *Don Juan Triumphant*?" Christine asked, thinking to please him so that he would not harm her.

"You must never ask me that," he said in a gloomy voice. "I will play you something by Mozart, if you like. But my *Don Juan*, Christine—its sound is like fire. There is some music that is so terrible that it harms all those who hear it. Let us sing something from another opera, Christine."

He led her to another room with a piano. He began to play.

Christine had no choice but to sing. The Phantom started the duet from the opera *Othello*. She sang the part of Desdemona, although she was terrified. The Phantom sang with love, but with jealousy and hatred. He sang as if he were the murderous Othello himself.

Christine was desperate now to see the face of the man beneath this hideous mask. She wanted to see the person whose voice this was. Still singing, she slowly stepped closer to the Phantom... then closer still.

Then, with a swift move, she snatched the mask away.

The Phantom threw back his head with a heart-stopping cry of grief and rage.

Christine gasped in horror. He looked like death. She stepped back, then fell to her knees as Erik came toward her.

Erik leaned over Christine. "Look! You want to see?" Erik cried. "See! Feast your eyes on my cursed ugliness! Look at Erik's face! Now you

She Snatched the Mask Away.

know the face of the voice! When a woman has seen me, as you have, she belongs to me. Forever!"

Christine turned her head away. "Please..." she begged.

Erik grabbed her hair. He twisted her head so that she had to face him. "Ah, I frighten you, do I? Perhaps you think this is another mask?" he snarled. "Tear it off as you did the other! Come! Give me your hands!" he raged, pulling her hands and pressing her fingers into his awful face.

"It is a dead thing that loves you and will never, never leave you! I am crying, crying for you, Christine. You have torn off my mask and so can never leave me!" he shouted.

Christine cried out and tried to wrench herself from his grasp, but Erik held her tightly by the hands.

"Now that you have seen me, I shall keep you here!"

Erik let go of Christine at last. She was sobbing. He left the room.

Soon, Christine heard Erik playing the organ. She knew he must be playing his own music, his *Don Juan Triumphant*, the music sounded like one long, awful, magnificent cry. The music drew Christine to it. She opened the door to the room with the organ. Erik stopped playing. He stood up as Christine came in.

"Erik," she said, trying to be brave, "show me your face without fear! If ever again I tremble when I look at you, it will be because I am thinking of your beautiful music!"

Erik turned toward Christine. He knelt at her feet. He did not see that Christine had closed her eyes. She could not stand to see his horrifying face. But she knew she must somehow keep him from hurting her now.

Erik kept Christine hidden in his underground world for days. She did all she could to get him to free her. She tried

A Carriage Waited for Them.

to make him think that he did not need to keep her there.

"If you let me go, I will come back to see you," she promised.

Slowly, he began to believe her. He took her walking beside the underground lake, and he rowed her around the lake in his boat. One day he showed her a road with gates that led to the Rue Scribe, the street next to the Opera House.

A carriage waited for them. It took them for a drive through Paris. For two nights they did this. On the second night, the night they drove past the racetrack, Christine did see Raoul standing by the roadside. She did want to call out to him then. But she did not dare show Erik her feelings for Raoul, for fear that Erik would hate Raoul—or worse.

Christine found herself filled with horror for Erik, but also with pity.

At last, Erik told Christine that he would set her free.

"I will come back!" she told him. But she knew she never wanted to return—not ever.

Erik took out a gold ring. He gave her the ring. "I set you free, Christine, but only for so long as this ring is on your finger. As long as you keep it, you will be safe from all danger. Erik will remain your friend. But if you ever part with it, Erik will have his revenge!"

He turned and left Christine alone at the Rue Scribe, where she could walk back to the upper world again.

She never wanted to see Erik again. But it was not his threats that would make her go to him. It was the pitiful sob she heard as she walked away from him and his dark world.

"Poor Erik!" she said, putting his ring on her finger.

She could not hate him, for he loved her. But terror filled her when she thought of having to go to him again. If she did, would she ever return again to the world above?

"Erik Will Have His Revenge!"

CHAPTER 10

The Phantom Strikes

On the rooftop of the Opera House, Raoul sat with Christine, the statue of Apollo behind them. Raoul tried to make sense of all she had told him.

"Why is it that you had been free from Erik for only a few hours before you returned to him? Remember the masked ball!" Raoul said.

"Yes, and do you remember the time that I spent with you then, Raoul? That put us both in great danger," Christine said, looking at him.

"I doubted your love for me," he told her.

"Do you doubt it still, Raoul? Then know that each of my visits to Erik made my horror of him grow stronger. And instead of calming him as I had hoped, each visit made his madness worse! I am so frightened!"

"But do you love me, Christine?"

She put her trembling arms around Raoul. "If I did not love you, I would not give you this!" She kissed him, but as she did, lightning flashed. Rain pelted them. Christine and Raoul jumped up. From the dome of the roof above them, it seemed that red eyes stared at them from next to the statue of Apollo.

They ran from the storm—and from those eyes.

They did not stop running until they were inside the Opera House. There was no performance that night, and the house was empty. Suddenly, a small man stood before them, blocking the stairway.

Raoul hesitated, looking at the stranger.

"Go Away Quickly!"

"No, not this way!" the man said. He pointed to another hall. "Quick! Go away quickly!"

Christine pulled Raoul with her.

"Who is that man? What is he doing here?" Raoul asked.

"Everyone knows him only as the Persian. He is always in the Opera House," Christine replied.

"Those eyes on the roof—was that Erik?" Raoul asked.

"You are getting like me now, seeing him everywhere! But it could not have been Erik. He is working on his opera and not thinking of us. It must have been the lightning, glinting off the statue on the dome," Christine said.

"We should leave Paris at once. Why wait for tomorrow? He may have heard us tonight," Raoul said.

"No, no, he is working, I tell you," Christine said. "And I promised them that I would sing an important role at the opera tonight."

"If you're so sure he is not watching us, why do you keep looking back?" Raoul asked.

"Come to my dressing room," Christine said. "Erik gave me his word not to hide behind the walls of my dressing room again. That room and my bedroom on the underground lake are for me only."

Raoul followed Christine into her dressing room. He glanced around at the costumes Christine wore in the operas, and the mirror that covered one wall. "How can you have gone from this room into that dark passage, Christine?"

Raoul moved to examine the mirror, but Christine stopped him.

"Don't. The mirror might carry me away again. Then I would have go to the lake and call for Erik."

"Would he hear you?" Raoul asked.

"Erik will hear me wherever I call him. He

"Why Do You Keep Looking Back?"

told me so. He does things that no other man can do. He knows things which nobody in the world knows."

Raoul was beginning to believe this was true. Erik was more like a phantom than a man.

"I shall be here at twelve tomorrow night," Raoul told Christine, taking her hand. "I shall keep my promise and take you away. We will leave Erik waiting for you by the lake."

Christine smiled. But then she looked down at her hand in Raoul's, and she turned pale.

She gasped. "The gold ring Erik gave me! It is gone!"

They both looked everywhere for the ring, but they could not find it.

"It was when I kissed you," Christine said. "The ring must have slipped from my finger and dropped into the street! We can never find it!"

"Let us run away at once," Raoul insisted once more.

She hesitated. He thought she was going to

say yes, but she shook her head. Raoul knew then that her pity for Erik would make her stay and sing for him, as she had said she would.

"No! It must be tomorrow as we promised!" she said.

Christine left him, rubbing her fingers, as though she hoped that doing so would bring the ring back to her hand.

Raoul went home, greatly worried. She had lost the ring that Erik had said would keep her safe. Tomorrow she would leave Paris. But was she safe until then?

"If I don't save her," he murmured, "she is lost. But I shall save her!"

The next morning, Count Philippe sent for Raoul. Raoul came into the breakfast room silent and gloomy, thinking of how he could leave Paris with Christine.

Count Philippe handed Raoul a copy of the morning newspaper.

"You Cannot Marry Her!"

"Read that!" said the count, pointing to a story that reported that Raoul and Christine had been seen running into the Opera House during the storm.

"What of it?" said Raoul. "It is just gossip. There are rumors that I want to marry Christine. So what? What if I do?"

"Raoul, you are making our family look bad!" said the count, pounding the table. "This Christine is only an opera singer. You cannot marry her!"

"I leave Paris tonight with Christine," Raoul answered defiantly. "So this is good-bye, Philippe."

"You will not do anything so foolish as this!" the count raged. "You have a career to think of! And I shall know how to stop you!"

"Good-bye, Philippe," Raoul said again firmly, and left the room.

Raoul spent the day getting ready to leave. He went out to hire a carriage and coachman.

He had to pack, and he had to get money for the trip. They would travel by carriage instead of by train, just in case Philippe did try to stop them.

At nine o'clock, Raoul arrived at the Opera in a carriage. It was drawn by two powerful horses. He left his carriage in front of the Opera House, near other carriages that stood below the wide stone steps that led into the huge building.

The opera *Faust* was to be sung that night, and the house was full. Every seat had been sold. Count Philippe sat alone in his box. He stared at the stage and frowned. His thoughts were someplace else.

Raoul did not go to sit next to his brother. Instead, he bought a ticket for one of the seats below.

Christine sang with all her heart and soul. In the last act, when she began the opera's song to the angels, she made everyone feel as if they, too, had wings. Her voice soared, as if she was reaching for the very Heaven she sang about.

Song to the Angels

"Holy angel, in Heaven blessed." Christine sang, her arms stretched out, her silky hair falling over her shoulders. "My spirit longs with thee to rest!"

Suddenly the stage went dark! Everyone gasped. Then the gaslights lit the stage again.

But Christine was not there!

CHAPTER 11

Christine! Christine!

The other singers and dancers rushed from the sides of the stage to the spot where Christine had been standing and singing. Where had she gone?

Count Philippe sprang to his feet.

Raoul cried out and ran for the stage, and Count Philippe left his box. The curtain came down on the stage. Slowly, the curtain rose again and one of the opera managers stepped out.

"Ladies and gentlemen," the manager announced, "Christine Daaé has disappeared!

Had the Phantom Carried Her Away?

But nobody knows how!"

Raoul's first thought was that Erik had done this. He no longer doubted the ghostly powers of the Angel of Music. Raoul rushed onto the stage, despair in his heart.

"Christine! Christine!" Raoul called out. Had the Phantom once again carried her away to his dark realm?

Raoul thought he heard Christine's screams through the wooden boards of the stage. He bent forward and listened. But how could he follow her? He could find no way to get under the stage from where he was.

"Christine!" Raoul called again. "Why don't you answer?"

How had Erik dragged Christine away? Horrible thoughts came into Raoul's mind. Erik must have learned that Christine had planned to leave. And Erik had acted before she could safely get away from Paris.

Raoul ran to Christine's dressing room.

Bitter tears burned his eyes. He looked around the room, searching for a way to find her.

He saw Christine's clothes scattered over the furniture. Oh, why had she not left with him last night? Why had she wanted to sing tonight, just because she had promised to? Just because she pitied Erik?

Raoul turned to the mirror that took up one wall of Christine's dressing room. Christine had said this was the way to Erik. Raoul pushed and pressed at the mirror, but the mirror did not move. Did the mirror only open if he said the right words?

Raoul rushed from the dressing room. He stopped the first person he saw, a woman who worked in the Opera House.

"I beg your pardon, madam, can you tell me how to get to the underground lake under the Opera?"

The old woman shrugged. "I know there is a

The Mirror Did Not Move.

lake under the Opera, but I don't know which door leads to it. I have never been there!"

Raoul ran from her. He rushed through the Opera House, looking for someone to help him. He found himself once more on the stage. He stopped, his heart thumping, when he saw a group of men, all in formal evening clothes.

The men all seemed to be talking at once. Raoul saw that one of the men was an Opera House manager, Monsieur Richard. He stood with a man in police uniform. No one knew what had happened to Christine.

As Raoul was about to approach the men, he felt a hand on his shoulder. A chill spread up his spine.

"Erik's secrets concern no one but himself!" a voice next to Raoul said in a sharp whisper.

Raoul turned around with a gasp.

The man with the hand on Raoul's shoulder was the same man he had seen when he was coming down from the roof with Christine. This man Christine had called the Persian.

The Persian hurried away, leaving Raoul alone again.

The voices of the group of men grew louder. Raoul turned back to them.

"The Phantom!" said one of the Opera House managers. "Could it be a ghost who talks in Box Five, who makes the chandelier fall, and who makes Christine disappear?"

Raoul stepped forward. "I am sure that Christine Daaé was carried off by an angel," Raoul said, speaking to the policemen. "And I can tell you his name. And where he lives. The angel is called Erik, he lives in the Opera House, and he is the Angel of Music!"

"The Angel of Music! Really!" one policeman said. He turned to the Opera House managers. "Do you have an Angel of Music here?" he asked them.

The managers, Monsieur Richard and Monsieur Moncharmin, shook their heads, staring at Raoul.

"They Are Both a Real Man Named Erik."

"But you have heard of the Phantom of the Opera," Raoul said, stepping forward. "And I tell you that the Opera ghost and the Angel of Music are the same. They are both a real man named Erik."

"Are you making fun of the law? What is all this about the Opera ghost?" asked the policeman.

"Oh, let us tell him everything!" Monsieur Moncharmin said, looking at Monsieur Richard.

The policeman glanced from one man to the other and ran a hand through his hair. Then he looked at Raoul. "You believe," the policeman said to Raoul, "that Christine Daaé has been carried off by a man named Erik?"

"I know it sounds mad, but I beg you to believe that I am telling the truth," Raoul said. "The safety of the person dearest to me in the world is at stake. I will try to be brief, for every moment is valuable. But I will tell you what I know about the Phantom of the Opera."

Raoul told them all he knew of Erik. He

talked about the mirror and Christine's singing lessons. He told them of the gold ring that Christine had lost. He watched the faces of the men as he spoke. He knew they thought he had lost his mind, that they did not believe him.

Before Raoul could finish his story, a man dressed in a huge coat and a tall hat hurried over. The man spoke in a whisper, as if telling something important to the policeman.

The policeman turned to Raoul.

"Monsieur, we have talked enough about the ghost," the policeman said. "We will now talk about yourself a little. Is it true, what I have just heard, that you were to take Miss Daaé away tonight after the performance?"

"Yes, sir," Raoul answered.

"All your arrangements were made? You have had a carriage waiting, and it is still outside waiting for you now, is it not?"

"Yes, sir," Raoul said again. He frowned. Why so many questions? They should be

"We Will Now Talk About You."

searching for Christine and for Erik!

"Did you know that there was another carriage next to yours?" the policeman asked. "A carriage that belongs to your brother, the count."

"What has this to do with anything?" Raoul demanded.

"Was not your brother, the count, opposed to your going away with Christine Daaé? Well, it seems that your brother has outsmarted you! He has carried off Christine Daaé!"

"Impossible!" cried Raoul, pressing his hand to his head.

"Right after Christine disappeared—and we still have to find out how the count did that—Count Philippe ran to his carriage and sped across Paris at a galloping pace. He has left Paris by the Brussels road."

"Then I shall catch them!" Raoul said. He turned and ran for the door.

As soon as Raoul left the stage and stepped into a dark hall, a man blocked his way.

"Where are you going so fast?" asked the man.

"It's you again!" Raoul cried out. "You who know Erik's secrets and don't want me to speak of them. Just who are you, Persian?"

He Was Called the Persian.

CHAPTER 12

The Persian

Raoul remembered that Christine had said that nothing was known about this man except that he was called the Persian.

The man was short, with dark skin and eyes of jade green, and he wore a cap.

"I hope you have not betrayed Erik's secret," the Persian said.

"And why should I hesitate to betray that monster, sir?" Raoul replied. "Is he your friend, by any chance?"

"I hope you said nothing about Erik, sir,

because Erik's secret is also Christine's secret. To talk about one is to talk about the other!"

Raoul became more anxious. "You seem to know about many things that interest me. But I have no time to listen to you!" Raoul told the mysterious man.

"But where are you going to so fast?" the Persian asked.

"Can you not guess? To rescue Christine," Raoul answered.

"Then, sir, stay here, for Christine is here. With Erik!" the Persian said.

"How do you know?" Raoul asked him.

"I was watching. No one in the world but Erik could take anyone away like that!" the Persian said with a deep sigh. "I know that monster's touch!"

"You know him, then?" Raoul asked, surprised.

The Persian did not reply, but sighed deeply. He looked keenly at Raoul once

"I Know That Monster's Touch!"

again. Then he nodded.

"Sir, I do not know if you mean to do any good, but can you do anything to help me? To help Christine?" Raoul pleaded.

"I think so, and that is why I spoke to you," the Persian said.

"What can you do?" Raoul asked. "I will try to take you to her—and to him," the Persian said, his green eyes shining.

"If you can do that, sir, I will owe you my life!" Raoul said. "But the police just told me that Christine has been carried off by my brother, Count Philippe."

"I don't believe that," the Persian said, shaking his head. "There are ways of carrying people off, and then there are ways. Count Philippe has never, as far as I know, had anything to do with such witchcraft as this."

"Then let us leave at once!" Raoul said. "I put myself in your hands! How can I not believe you, when you are the only one to believe me, and when you are the only one not to smile when Erik's name is spoken?"

Raoul grabbed the Persian's hands. They were ice-cold.

"Silence!" said the Persian, stopping and listening to the sounds in the Opera House. "We must not mention that name here. We do not want to call him to us here."

"Do you think he is nearby?" Raoul asked.

"He may be. Or he may be in his house near the lake," the Persian answered.

"So you know about that house too?" Raoul said, frowning.

"If he is not there, then he may be here, in this wall, in this floor, in this ceiling! We must be careful. Now, come!" the Persian said.

Picking up a small lantern that stood nearby, the Persian led Raoul down dark passages he had never seen before.

"What did you say to the policeman?" the Persian asked in a whisper, making sure the

Holding the Lantern High

candle flickering in the lantern was strong enough to light their way.

"I said that Christine had been taken by the Phantom of the Opera," Raoul said.

"And did he believe you?" the Persian asked.

Raoul shook his head. "No," he said.

"He thought you a madman?" the Persian said.

"Yes," Raoul answered.

"So much the better!" said the Persian.

Holding the lantern high, the Persian led Raoul up and down several staircases which Raoul had never seen. Soon the two men found themselves in front of a door that the Persian opened with a master key.

Then the Persian took Raoul through the door and into Christine's dressing room.

"How well you know the Opera, sir!" Raoul said.

"Not so well as the ghost does!" said the Persian grimly. Raoul watched as the

Persian set the lantern down carefully.

Closing the door quietly behind them, the Persian pulled out a pair of long pistols from his coat.

"Do you mean to fight a duel?" asked Raoul, looking at the pistols.

"Almost certainly we shall have to defend ourselves," said the Persian. He handed one of the pistols to Raoul, who took it quickly.

"You must be ready for everything, for we shall be resisting the most awful enemy that you can imagine. But you love Christine, do you not?" asked the Persian.

"I worship the ground she stands on!" Raoul said. "But you, sir, do not love her. Why are you ready to risk your life for her? You must hate Erik!"

"No, sir," said the Persian sadly, "I do not hate him. And I have forgiven him the harm which he has done me."

"I do not understand. You treat him as a

"Why Are You Ready to Risk Your Life?"

monster, you speak of his crime. He has done you harm and you have the same pity that I saw in Christine for him!" Raoul said.

The Persian did not answer. He got a chair. He set it against the wall opposite the great mirror that filled a whole wall. Setting the lantern closer for light, the Persian climbed on the chair and pressed his face to the wall. He seemed to be looking for something.

"Ah," he said, after a long search, "I have it!" He raised his finger above his head and pressed against part of the wall. Then he turned round and jumped off the chair.

The Persian ran across the dressing room and pressed a hand against the mirror.

"No, it is not yielding yet," the Persian muttered.

"Are we going out by the mirror?" asked Raoul. "Like Christine?"

"So you knew that Christine went out by that mirror?" asked the Persian.

"She did so before my eyes, sir! I was hidden behind the curtain and I saw her vanish into the mirror! I thought it was a mad dream."

"Or some new trick of the ghost's!" chuckled the Persian. He kept pressing on the mirror. "It takes some time to release the spring from inside the room," he continued. "It is different when you are behind the wall. Then the mirror turns at once and quickly."

"What spring?" asked Raoul.

"Why, the one that turns this entire wall. Surely you don't expect it moves by magic! If you watch, you will see the mirror first rise an inch or two, and then shift an inch or two from left to right. It will then spin from its center," the Persian explained.

"It's not turning!" said Raoul impatiently.

"Wait! It will. Unless something else has happened," added the Persian.

"Something else?" Raoul asked.

"The ghost may have blocked the way," the

"He Commands the Walls and the Doors."

Persian said.

"Why should he? He does not know we are coming this way!" Raoul said.

"I daresay he might think we may," the Persian answered.

"It's not turning!" Raoul said, frustrated now.

"We shall do all we can. But he may try to stop us! He commands the walls, the doors and the trapdoors," the Persian said.

"But he did not build these walls," Raoul said, frowning.

"Yes, sir, that is just what he did!" the Persian said.

Raoul looked at him. He started to ask him to explain this, but the Persian made a sign for him to be silent. He pointed to the mirror. The mirror seemed to shake. Their images reflected in the mirror by lamplight looked like a rippling sheet of water.

"You see, sir, that it is not turning!" Raoul said. "Let us go another way!"

"Tonight, there is no other," the Persian answered in a sad voice. He picked up the lantern again. "And now, look out! And be ready to fire your weapon."

Suddenly, the mirror turned. It turned as easily as one of the revolving doors one could see in the restaurants and hotels of Paris. The mirror turned, sweeping Raoul and the Persian around with it, propelling them from the light of the dressing room into the deepest darkness.

Suddenly, the Mirror Turned.

CHAPTER 13

Under the Opera

The Persian raised his pistol. Raoul did so as well.

"Keep your hand high and be ready to fire!" the Persian said again, in a warning tone.

The wall behind them closed again. They stood still. Raoul held his breath.

Raoul heard the Persian step forward. Light flared up from the lantern the Persian had carried through from the dressing room. Raoul saw that the floor, the walls and the ceiling were all made of wooden planks. Raoul remembered that the Persian had said that this secret passage had been built by the ghost himself.

The Persian put the lantern down, then felt around on the floor. Raoul heard a faint click. Then he saw a pale square of light in the floor.

"Follow me and do all that I do," the Persian whispered.

Raoul turned to the square of light. The Persian slipped into the square opening, hung by his hands from the rim and then slid into the cellar below.

Raoul trusted the Persian, for the small man had sounded as if he, too, knew that Erik was a monster. And if the Persian had meant any harm, he would not have given Raoul a pistol. Besides, Raoul was determined to get to Christine. He, too, slipped into the square hole and hung from the trapdoor opening with both hands.

"Let go!" said a voice.

Raoul dropped to the ground. Then he stood

The Faint Light Was Just Enough.

up. The faint light was just enough for Raoul to see the shapes of things around him.

They stood in one of the huge cellars under the Opera House. The Persian led Raoul from one giant underground cellar to the next. Raoul followed and wondered what he would have done without the Persian as his guide.

The lower they went, the more cautious the Persian became. He kept turning around to see if Raoul held his arm up as if always ready to fire.

In the fifth cellar, the Persian drew a deep breath. After telling Raoul to stay where he was, the Persian ran up a few steps of a staircase. A few minutes later, he came back.

"Will the ghost come after us?" Raoul asked.

"If he does come up behind us, we are at risk if we do not keep one head up! I know Erik too well to feel at all safe with him around," the Persian replied.

The Persian had hardly finished speaking

when out of the darkness a fiery face came toward them. It floated at a man's height, but with no body attached. The face looked like a flame in the shape of a man's face.

"It is not the ghost, but he may have sent it! Come, let us run!" said the Persian.

They fled down the long hall in front of them. After a few seconds, they stopped.

"The ghost doesn't often come this way," said the Persian. "This side of the Opera House is the long way to get to the lake and the house there. But perhaps the Phantom knows that we are after him!"

He turned his head and Raoul also turned to look. Raoul again saw the head of fire. It had followed them. It must have run also, perhaps faster than they did, for it seemed to be much nearer.

At the same time, they began to hear a strange noise. It sounded like thousands of fingernails scraping against a blackboard.

A Fiery Face Came Toward Them.

Raoul and the Persian stepped back, but the fiery face came at them. The eyes were round and glaring, the nose a little crooked and the mouth large, with a hanging lower lip.

How did that head glide through the darkness? How did it go so fast? And what was that scraping sound it brought with it?

The Persian and Raoul flattened themselves against the wall. They heard other sounds and saw other shadows move in the darkness, under the fiery face.

Raoul's hair stood on end. He knew what the other noises were. Rats. They came in a troop, hustled along by the fire, swifter than the waves that break over the shore at high tide.

The rats passed between Raoul's feet and started climbing up his legs. Raoul cried out in horror. He dropped his hands to push at the little legs and nails and claws and teeth.

Then the head of fire turned around. "Don't move! And whatever you do, don't come after me!

I am the rat-catcher! Let me pass, with my rats!" the head said.

The head of fire disappeared, vanished in the darkness. He left, dragging with him his rats, taking with him his lantern which he held up before him. It was the lantern that had made his head seem to glow with fire.

Raoul and the Persian both let out great sighs of relief.

"I ought to have remembered that Erik told me about the rat-catcher," said the Persian.

"Are we very far from the lake?" asked Raoul. "When we are at the lake, we can cross it and then call out to Christine!"

"We shall never cross that lake, for it is well guarded! I was almost killed there. So, never go near the lake. And if you hear the voice singing under the water, the siren's voice, do not listen! It will mean your death."

"But what are we here for then?" Raoul insisted. "If you can do nothing for Christine,

"Only One Way to Save Christine"

at least let me die for her!"

"We have only one way to save Christine, which is to enter the house without being seen by the Phantom."

"Is there any hope of that?" Raoul asked.

"Ah, if I did not have that hope, I would not have come to help you!" the Persian said.

"But how can one enter the house on the lake without crossing the lake?" Raoul asked.

"I will take you to a secret way into that house," the Persian said.

Raoul knew they must be very deep underground. He could still hear footsteps from above them in the Opera House, but these sounds soon faded into silence as they crept farther and farther, Raoul following the Persian's every step, the light from the lantern still flickering to guide their way to the secret entrance into the house.

They came upon a little staircase and started up, stopping at each step, peering into the darkness and the silence. Then the Persian motioned to Raoul to get on his knees. Both crawling on their knees, they reached a wall.

The Persian stopped and listened. He looked up and then down. His lantern sent a shaft of light through the boards under them. This seemed to trouble him.

With his free hand, the Persian felt along the wall. Raoul watched the Persian press against the wall, just as he had pressed against the mirror in Christine's dressing room. A stone moved back, leaving a hole in the wall.

The Persian took a tight grip on his pistol and made a sign for to Raoul to do the same.

Still on his knees, the Persian wiggled through the hole in the wall. Raoul followed him.

On the other side, the Persian lifted his lantern again, stooped forward, and looked down into another hole in the floor.

"I am going to hang by my hands from the

On Their Knees, They Reached a Wall.

edge of the hole and let myself down into the Phantom's house. You must do the same," the Persian said in a whisper. He then dropped through the hole.

Raoul heard a dull sound as the Persian's boots hit stone. Then Raoul dropped down into the hole.

"Hush!" said the Persian.

They stood motionless, listening. The darkness hung thick around them, the silence heavy and frightening.

The Persian lifted his lantern. He looked up, searching for the hole through which they had fallen.

"Oh no!" the Persian groaned. "The hole has closed in on itself!"

Raoul looked around.

They were in the middle of a small six-cornered room. All the sides were covered with mirrors from top to bottom. Around the room, they could see trees from the theater stage.

They seemed to be made of metal. Their branches ran up to the ceiling.

"We have dropped into the Phantom's torture chamber!" the Persian said, wiping the sweat from his forehead.

Suddenly, Raoul heard a noise from behind the mirror on the left. It sounded like a door opening and shutting in a room next to this one.

Then he heard a dull moan. And someone spoke.

"You must make your choice! The wedding song or the funeral song!" said the Phantom.

Raoul knew they must be inside the house near the underground lake.

And then Raoul heard Christine's voice.

"You Are Afraid of Me!" Erik Exclaimed.

CHAPTER 14

Christine Must Choose

In the house beside the underground lake, Christine moaned. Erik stood next to her.

"You must make a choice," he said again. "My opera *Don Juan Triumphant* is finished. Now I want to live like everybody else. I want to have a wife. I have made a mask so people will not even turn around in the streets to look at me. You will be the happiest of women. And we will sing together!"

Christine began to cry.

"You are afraid of me!" Erik exclaimed. Why

could he not understand that imprisoning her was so terrifying? "And yet I am not really wicked," he told her. "Love me and you will see! If you loved me, I would do anything you please."

"Yes or no!" he demanded then. "If your answer is no, everybody will be dead and buried!"

Christine cringed in fear. She could not answer him. She could only cry with fright. Erik dropped to his knees in front of her.

"Why do you cry? You know it gives me pain to see you cry!" Erik moaned.

Still, Christine could not find her voice to answer him.

Suddenly a bell rang. Erik stood up, wide-eyed with suspicion.

"Somebody is ringing at my door!" Erik whispered. "Who has come bothering me now? Wait for me here," he ordered Christine. Then he stalked out of the room, closing the door behind him.

He Stalked Out of the Room.

"Christine! Christine!" a voice called.

Christine glanced around. Could it be Raoul calling to her?

"I am dreaming!" Christine said aloud, her voice weak.

"Christine, it is Raoul!" the voice called again from behind the wall.

"Raoul?" Christine whispered. "I must be dreaming!"

"It is not a dream! Christine, trust me! We are here to save you. But be careful! When you hear the Phantom, warn us!" Raoul said from behind the wall.

Christine trembled at the thought of Erik finding out where Raoul was hiding.

"Erik has gone mad. He will kill everybody and himself if I do not agree to become his wife," Christine told Raoul. "He has given me until eleven o'clock tomorrow night—and then I must choose. And if I do not choose him, everyone will die!"

"Can you tell us where Erik is?" Raoul asked.

"He must have left the house," Christine answered.

"Can you make sure?" Raoul said from behind the wall.

"No. I am tied to a wall. I cannot move. But where are you?" asked Christine. "There are only two doors to the room I am in. A door that Erik uses to come and go, and another which he says is the door of the torture chamber!"

"Christine, that is where we are! But we cannot see or open the door from this side," Raoul told her.

"Oh, if I could only drag myself there, I could knock at the door and that would tell you where it is," Christine said. She tried desperately to free herself from the ropes.

"Is there a lock on the door?" Raoul asked.

"Yes—and I know where the key is," Christine said as she struggled to free herself.

Heavy Footsteps Were Coming Closer.

"Erik keeps the key in a small leather bag near the organ. Oh, Raoul—go back by the way you came! There must be a reason why that room is called a torture chamber! You must not stay!"

"Christine," Raoul replied, "we will go from here together—or die together!"

"Erik will not let me die until eleven o'clock tomorrow night," Christine said.

"Christine! Remember that Erik loves you! Smile at him. Ask him to set you free. Tell him that it hurts your wrists to be tied," Raoul instructed her.

"Hush!" Christine warned. "I hear something. It is Erik! Go away!"

Heavy footsteps were coming closer. Then Erik came into the room. Christine cried out in terror. Erik had taken off his mask!

"Why did you cry out?" Erik asked.

"I am in pain, Erik." Christine wept softly.

"I feared I had frightened you," Erik said,

coming closer to her.

"Untie my hands—please?" Christine begged.

Erik shook his head. "You will try to harm yourself—or try to leave," he answered her.

"You have given me until eleven o'clock tomorrow night, Erik. What harm could it do until then?" Christine asked.

"You are right." He untied her. "There, you're free now. Oh, my poor Christine. Look at your wrists. I hurt you. That alone deserves death."

Erik went into the next room where the organ was. He began to play and sing. His voice sounded like thunder.

Christine slipped from the other room and crept closer to the organ. Without a sound, she reached out and took the bag with the keys in it. She turned away.

But then the music stopped.

"What have you done with my bag?" Erik snarled.

Christine Crept Closer to the Organ.

CHAPTER 15

The Torture Begins

"So it was to take my bag of keys that you asked me to untie you!" Erik raged.

Christine turned and ran back into the other room toward the door that led to the torture chamber and Raoul.

"Why do you run from me?" Erik called as he followed her. "Give me back my bag! Don't you know that is the bag of life and death?"

"Listen to me, Erik," cried Christine. "As long as we are going to be together, what does this little bag matter to you?"

"You know there are only two keys in that bag. What do you want with it?" Erik demanded.

"I want to see the room I have never seen," Christine said. She tried to sound lighthearted, as if it was not really important.

But her trick did not fool Erik.

"I don't like nosy people," Erik told her. "Give me back my bag! Leave the keys alone!"

He grabbed Christine's wrist. She cried in pain. From behind the wall, Raoul shouted in anger.

"What was that?" Erik said, his head snapping up in surprise.

"I heard nothing," Christine said.

"I thought I heard a cry."

"I cried out because you hurt me! I heard nothing else," Christine persisted.

"Liar!" Erik boomed. "There is someone hiding in the torture chamber!"

"There is no one there!" Christine insisted, fearing she might lose her courage.

"We Need Only Pull Back This Curtain."

"Perhaps the man you want to marry is there?" Erik asked, guessing.

"I don't want to marry anybody. You know I don't," Christine cried out in fear.

Erik laughed an evil laugh. "Well, it won't take long to find out. You see, Christine, my love, we need not open the door to see what is happening in the torture chamber. We need only pull back this black curtain and put out the light in this room!" he sneered. "Then, we can see into the torture chamber through this little window."

"No! I'm afraid of the dark!" she cried, "I don't care about that room now! You're always frightening me! I don't care about that room."

Erik put out the light. Christine whimpered in terror as the room went black.

He kept hold of Christine's wrist as he yanked back a curtain. It was a window into the torture chamber!

She saw Raoul in the other room. Raoul

glanced around in surprise at the sound. A short, dark man stood next to Raoul. It was the Persian.

"I told you there was someone!" Erik burst out in anger. "Do you see the window now? Well, the men behind the wall can't see it! But now you will see the tortures!"

Christine screamed, desperately struggling to free herself from Erik's grip.

"What do you see in the room, Christine?" Erik taunted her.

Christine blinked, and looked hard. "I see trees," she answered, frightened. But she continued bravely. "You must be a great artist to have built this," she said, trying to make Erik think of anything except Raoul.

"Look at the picture I've created in there! Do you see any birds?" Erik asked.

"No, I do not," Christine said.

"But look again at my metal trees! I've made them so lifelike. You could say I

"I See Trees," She Answered.

created a little theater in there! You saw branches. Wouldn't you say a man can be hanged from them? And you can be the audience for my little play."

Suddenly, Erik shifted his eyes to hers. "But I am tired of it," he moaned. "I want to have a real house and a wife, like anybody else. My dear Christine—are you listening to me? Tell me you love me!" Erik begged her.

Christine could not utter a sound. He made no sense. She knew he must be mad.

"No, you don't love me. But you will! We could have wonderful times together. I can make you laugh, you know. I can make my voice come from other places. But you don't believe me? Listen!" Erik went on.

Christine knew Erik was trying to make her lose interest in the torture chamber. She could think only of Raoul and the danger he was in.

"Put out the light in the other room," she pleaded in the gentlest tone she could.

She knew the light must mean something terrible—it had made Erik smile that awful smile she had seen so many times.

Erik did not listen to her. He rambled on in his madness.

"Here, I raise my mask a little. You see my lips, such as I have. They're not moving! And yet you hear my voice. Where do you hear it? From the left? From the right?"

"And now it is in Madam Carlotta's throat, singing like a frog! Now it is on a chair in the ghost's box. It says Madam Carlotta is singing tonight to bring the chandelier down!" Erik said. His lips were not moving.

"Aha! Where is Erik's voice now? Listen, Christine, darling! It is behind the door of the torture chamber! It is I in the torture chamber! And I say: Woe to those who come to investigate the torture chamber!" Erik let out a wild wicked laugh.

Christine looked around. Erik's horrible

"It Is Getting Hot in Here!" Christine Cried.

voice seemed to be everywhere.

"Erik!" Christine cried in alarm. "It is getting hot in here!"

"Oh, yes! The heat is past what anyone can stand!" Erik replied, sounding pleased.

"But what does that mean?" Christine begged. Then she looked into the torture chamber and cried out. "The wall is so hot! It is burning!"

"I will tell you, Christine. It is because of my forest! Didn't you see it is a tropical forest?" Erik told her with an evil laugh.

Christine cried out, watching in terror as Raoul shouted, banging hard against the walls as they grew hotter. The Persian tried to stop him. Erik's laughter filled the house.

Erik dragged Christine from the room, slamming the door behind them, hoping Raoul and the Persian would be trapped in the heat of the underground metal forest!

CHAPTER 16

Mirror, Mirror!

Raoul glanced up at the ceiling, trying to figure out a plan. He rubbed his forehead as if to drive away a bad dream. As gaslights flickered, Raoul could see how the mirrors on the walls were broken and scratched. Others must have kicked against these mirrors when they, too, were trapped here, he thought.

The gaslight was making the room grow hotter now. Sweat trickled down Raoul's face.

"Christine!" Raoul cried out. He turned to the Persian. "We must get out!"

"We Must Get Out!"

"We must find the door to leave the room!" the Persian said. "We must search for it!"

The Persian began to feel along the mirrors, pressing on them to try to open a door as he had in Christine's dressing room. He felt along the top, as high up as he could reach.

They felt as if they were roasting in that glowing metal forest.

"All these mirrors are sending out too much heat!" Raoul called to the Persian. "Do you think you will find another metal spring soon? If it takes much longer, we shall surely be roasted alive!"

"You must hold out!" the Persian shouted.

"At least the Phantom has given Christine until eleven tomorrow night," Raoul replied. He, too, felt along the mirrors to help the Persian. They moved quickly around the room, gulping hot air that nearly made them faint.

The Persian kept searching for a hidden door. He found nothing.

They took off their coats and shirts, baring their skin to the heat. They had to quickly put their coats back on again.

"Oh, how thirsty I am!" Raoul cried out.

They kept hunting for a spring to reveal the hidden door. The Persian told Raoul to hold the pistols as if ready to fire, while he went on looking for the door.

Suddenly, they heard a lion roaring.

"There is a lion quite close! If he roars again, I will fire!" Raoul said.

The roaring grew louder. Raoul aimed and fired the pistol, but he only shattered a mirror.

"Erik must have created a trick with a lion's roar," the Persian said. "Erik! Erik!" he shouted out.

There was no answer. Tired, the Persian sat down beside Raoul. They panted with fatigue,
wiping the sweat from their brows.

Then Raoul sat up and pointed at a mirror. He wondered if what he saw was real.

"Look!" the Persian Cried Out.

It looked as if they could see water.

"Water!" Raoul said, dragging himself towards the mirror.

"It's another trick of the mirrors!" the Persian warned him. The Persian picked up the lantern. Its candle still burned strong.

Then they heard water. They heard rain, but no rain fell.

"Erik has a long narrow box with wooden and metal pegs inside it. As the stones fall down inside the box they sound like a rain-storm," the Persian explained to Raoul, to show him how Erik could create trick sounds.

When Raoul reached the mirror, he touched the glass. It was burning hot! He rolled away with a cry.

"Look!" the Persian cried out. "On the floor next to you! A black-headed nail! That must be the spring that opens the door."

The Persian crawled over to Raoul and pressed down on the nail. It moved! But instead of a door opening in the wall, a trapdoor opened in the floor. Cool air rushed up at them from the black hole below. Raoul and the Persian bent over the square of darkness.

"Could there be water to drink down there?" the Persian wondered aloud. He put his arm down into the darkness. "I can feel the beginning of a stone staircase—yes, it is stairs leading into the cellar. But wait—this may be a new trick! Let me go first." He took the lantern and carefully began to climb down.

Raoul followed the Persian down a winding staircase. It was cool and dark. The lake could not be far away, Raoul was certain.

They soon reached the bottom of the stairs. The Persian held up the lantern so they could see. They saw a small room full of wooden barrels.

They were in Erik's cellar.

"Erik must keep his drinking water here," the Persian said.

"This May Be a New Trick!"

Raoul thumped on a barrel. After half lifting the lid to make sure it was full, he got down on his knees and used the blade of a small knife he had in his pocket, carving a hole into the wood so they could drink.

"Barrels! Barrels! Any barrels to sell?" a voice boomed.

"That's odd! It sounds as if the barrels are talking!" Raoul wondered aloud.

He turned back to the open barrel. There was powder flowing out of it. "What's this? This isn't water!" Raoul cried.

He put his hands into the powder. Then he moved his hands close to the lantern.

The Persian tossed away the lantern. It broke and was snuffed out, leaving them now in darkness.

"What I saw in your hands was gunpowder!" the Persian shouted. "We almost blew ourselves up by bringing it close to the lantern's flame!"

CHAPTER 17

Blown Up!

Raoul knew now what Erik had meant when he said to Christine, "If your answer is no, everybody will be dead and buried!"

Erik had given Christine until eleven o'clock the next night. He had chosen his time well. There would be many people there.

And Erik would surely blow up everyone during the opera if Christine said no! Erik would go to his death along with the richest men and women of Paris, all in their jewels and finery.

They Heard a Cracking Sound.

They would all be buried under the ruins of the Paris Opera!

But what else could Christine say but no? Would she not choose death, rather than be married to the Phantom? Christine knew nothing about the gunpowder hidden under the Opera House.

"Eleven o'clock tomorrow evening!" Raoul said. They must find a way to stop Erik at once.

"What is the time now?" asked the Persian.

What was the time, Raoul wondered as well. How long had they been trapped in that room of heat and mirrors? It was too dark to see the hands on his pocket watch. Was it already close to eleven o'clock on the next evening?

Then they heard a cracking sound.

"Did you hear that?" the Persian whispered. "Like the sound of a machine? Perhaps it's a machine he has set up to cause an explosion!"

Raoul and the Persian began to yell. Fear drove them on. They stumbled back up the stone staircase, rushing back to the room of mirrors and heat.

They found the trapdoor still open, but everything was now as dark as the room of mirrors had been.

"Christine!" Raoul shouted, hoping to warn her about the gunpowder.

No one answered.

"If only we could see your watch!" said the Persian.

"I tried," Raoul answered. "But I cannot see the time. Wait—I know what I can do."

Raoul smashed the glass of his watch and felt its hands with his fingertips.

"I am not sure—but I think by the space between the hands, it might be just eleven o'clock now! But is it eleven o'clock in the morning or the evening? Might we still have twelve hours before us?" Raoul said.

"Hush!" said the Persian. "I hear footsteps in the next room."

Raoul Smashed the Glass of His Watch.

Raoul heard them, too. They held their breath. Then someone tapped against the wall.

"Raoul! Raoul!" It was Christine calling out!

"Christine!" Raoul cried.

Christine was crying. "I was not sure I would find you alive," she gasped. "Erik has been terrible! He wants me to tell him I will marry him! I told him I would if he would take me back to the torture chamber! But he would not do that. And he makes threats against all of Paris. After hours and hours of this, he says he has left me alone for the last time to think about my choice!" Christine called to Raoul, her voice muffled by the wall.

His heart raced. "Hours and hours? What is the time now?" he shouted. "What is the time, Christine?"

"It is almost eleven o'clock! Five minutes until eleven!" Christine warned them.

Her voice trembled. "He is quite mad! He pleads with me, then he threatens me. He tore off his mask. Then he told me the terribly strange way that I had to give him my answer! He says I am to twist the bronze scorpion statue. He keeps it in a box. I am to twist it for yes! Or I am to twist a bronze grasshopper there to mean no! And now he has gone off to throw the keys to the torture chamber into the lake!" Christine went on, desperately.

The Persian grabbed hold of Raoul's arm. "A grasshopper? It would hop—and with it, many members of the human race! There is no doubt that this mechanical grasshopper controls a machine! A machine that will blow up the gunpowder we saw!" the Persian said.

"Christine, you must turn the scorpion," Raoul called to her. Then he told her about the gunpowder and the Persian's guess.

There was a silent pause.

"Wait! Don't touch it!" the Persian now shouted. "I know Erik, and that monster has lied before. What if it is the *scorpion* that will

"I Shall Blow Up Everything!"

blow everything up? After all, why isn't Erik here? Perhaps he is someplace else, waiting for the whole Opera House to explode!"

"He is coming!" cried Christine. "I hear him!"

Raoul and the Persian heard Erik's steps, too.

"Erik! It is I!" the Persian cried out. "Do you know me?"

"So you are not dead in there?" Erik shouted back. "Well, then, keep quiet or I shall blow up everything at once!" Erik threatened.

Raoul and the Persian heard steps again. Then again they heard Erik's voice.

"Christine!" he said. "You have not touched the scorpion. You have not touched the grasshopper. But it is not too late." His voice was almost too calm.

"If you turn the grasshopper, we shall all be blown up. There is enough gunpowder under our feet to blow up a quarter of Paris. If you turn the grasshopper, it is the end for all of us.

If you turn the scorpion, all the gunpowder will be soaked with water," Erik said.

Erik paused for a moment. Then he began to speak again.

"If, in two minutes, Christine, you have not turned the scorpion, *I shall turn the grasshopper*! And the grasshopper, I tell you, hops high!"

There was a terrible silence again. Raoul knew there was nothing left to do now but pray. He got down on his knees. Silently he prayed.

Erik called out. "The two minutes are past. Good-bye, Christine."

"Erik!" cried Christine, "do you swear to me that the scorpion is the one to turn?"

"Yes. But you won't turn the scorpion! So I must turn the grasshopper!"

"But Erik! See! I *have* turned the scorpion!" Christine said, her voice pleading with him.

Raoul waited, sure he would find himself in fragments amid a great thunder of the gunpowder going off! He felt something crack under his

"I Have Turned the Scorpion!"

feet. Then he heard a hissing, like the sound of a gas lamp!

But it was not the hiss of fire. No—it was more like the sound of water. And then there came a gurgling sound.

Raoul and the Persian rushed to the trapdoor. Water was beginning to rise in the cellar below them. The gunpowder barrels began to float. Still thirsty, they went back down into the cellar. Water rose to the Persian's chin, and then to Raoul's. They drank. But still more water rose.

Turning, they climbed back up into the torture chamber. Now the water had begun to fill that room, too. If this went on, Raoul knew, the whole house on the lake would be flooded! Erik must turn off the water!

"Erik! Erik! There is water enough to destroy the gunpowder! Turn off the scorpion!" the Persian called to the Phantom.

But Erik did not reply. They heard nothing

but the water still rising. "Christine!" Raoul cried. "Christine!"

But Christine did not answer. There was no one in the next room to turn the scorpion again to stop the water! They were alone in the dark, with cold water rising around them.

"Christine!" Raoul shouted again.

He could no longer touch the floor. Now they had to swim. Water swept into the room. A great wave rushed Raoul and the Persian hard against the mirrors.

"Erik! Erik!" the Persian called out again to the Phantom. "I once saved your life! Remember! You were sentenced to death! If not for me, you would be dead now! Erik!"

Raoul caught hold of one of the branches of the metal trees. The Persian did the same.

The water was rising still higher.

"Swim! Swim for your life!" cried the Persian.

They fought the water with all their strength. Then suddenly they heard air going

They Slipped Beneath the Water.

out through a vent hole.

"Let us find the air hole! We can put our mouths against it!" the Persian said. He sounded as if he were losing his strength now.

But it was no use. Their fingers slid on the mirror walls as they tried to find an air hole. They struggled to keep swimming.

Then the Persian and Raoul slipped beneath the gurgling water.

CHAPTER 18

The End of the Ghost

Christine had heard Raoul and the Persian. She ran to Erik, her eyes open wide. She tried to speak calmly.

"Erik—I have said I will be your wife. I will not hurt myself ever. I will live with you. You said you would do anything to please me. And what would please me now is that you save Raoul and the Persian."

Erik nodded. "You did turn the scorpion. And you do not need two men both to be your husband."

"Save Raoul and the Persian."

"No, I do not. Now please, Erik. Stop the water—to please me," Christine pleaded.

Erik now turned the scorpion the other way. All the water was back in the lake. Then he opened the door into the torture chamber. The two men looked nearly gone. But Erik lifted the Persian and then Raoul.

Erik took the Persian back up to the Opera House. He laid him down, still alive where someone would find him.

But he would not set Raoul free—not after Erik had found Raoul's brother, Count Philippe, dead on the shore beside the underground lake.

Count Philippe had found his way into the cellars of the Opera house. He must have heard about the story of the Phantom, the story that was now all over Paris. And so Count Philippe had followed Raoul and come to the lake.

But Erik's deadly serpent kept watch there. It was Count Philippe who had knocked on Erik's door, but Erik had found the count already dead.

"It was an accident. A sad accident. He fell into the lake and died," Erik muttered.

Erik did not want Raoul to wake and learn about Count Philippe's death. But he could not keep Raoul in the house on the lake, because of Christine. Picking up Raoul's limp body, Erik carried him up to the Opera House cellar.

Erik chained Raoul to a wall where no one ever came.

Erik went back to Christine. He stared at her. There she was, in his house near the underground lake, obediently awaiting him. Erik went to her. She did not run from him. She stood still. He kissed her on the forehead. He sighed deeply. Even his own mother had never let him kiss her.

Erik fell at Christine's feet, crying. He heard her weeping softly.

Taking off his mask, Erik looked up. Christine wept for him. "Poor, unhappy Erik," she said, taking his hand.

"Believe in Me."

"I have tasted all the happiness the world can offer me!" Erik said. "I am ready to die for you. Believe in me!"

Erik stood up. He took out the plain gold ring he had once given her. She had lost it, but he had found it again.

"There. Take it! Take it for you...and him! This shall be my wedding present—from your poor Erik," he said, slipping the ring onto her finger.

"Because you have cried with me, because you let me kiss you, I will let you marry your young man," Erik said.

He stood up. "I am going to die—die of love. Of love for you."

Erik left suddenly. He went back to Raoul, and released him.

"Come with me," Erik ordered.

Raoul followed Erik back to the house. He rushed to Christine.

Erik watched them. "Christine, swear to

come back one night, when I am dead. Bury me secretly with the gold ring, which you are to wear until then. Do you swear it?" Erik pleaded.

Christine nodded, stepping away from Raoul. She kissed Erik on his forehead. Then she and Raoul slipped out.

Erik, alone, cried. But if Christine kept her promise, she would come back. Erik put his mask back on.

Erik would send word to the Persian to put a notice in the Paris papers, to tell Christine when to come back and bury him.

That was all.

Three weeks later, the notice was printed.

Erik is dead.

"Bury Me Secretly."

CHAPTER 19

The Angel of Music

Raoul and Christine were married. They decided to go where they could be far away from Paris. Christine felt she never wanted to sing again.

Before they left Paris, Christine and Raoul went to visit the Persian. They learned from him how he had first met Erik many years before in Persia.

Erik was the son of a great builder. But he had run away for he frightened his parents. He lived and worked in traveling fairs, and became known far and wide as the "living dead."

When his fame spread, the Persian was sent to bring him to Persia. There, the Shah of Persia had Erik build him a palace. Erik could do as he liked. There he perfected his secrets of hidden doors and passages, and other tricks.

Because Erik knew the palace secrets, the Shah ordered him killed. The Persian saved Erik, warning him and fleeing Persia with him.

They traveled all over. They came to Paris. He became a master builder on the Opera House. When it was finished, he hid himself behind his mask, living under the Opera House where he knew all the secret rooms and hidden passageways.

Raoul had learned of his brother's death. The newspapers told how Count Philippe had been found. The count had drowned, but how was a mystery.

Raoul was crushed by his brother's death. Now more than ever, he wanted to go away.

After Christine had seen the newspaper

notice, and had made good her promise to Erik, she and Raoul left Paris.

"Poor, unhappy Erik! Should we pity him? Should we curse him?" Christine asked Raoul. "He wanted only to be like everybody else. With an ordinary face, he could have been one of the greatest composers."

"He had a heart that could have held the world, but in the end, he had to be happy with no more than a cellar. We must pity the Phantom of the Opera," Raoul replied.

They left for the land where Christine had been a little girl, bringing Madam Valérius with them. Still sometimes Christine would hear the lonely echoes of her Angel of Music.

The Phantom lay now near the little well, the spot where he had first carried Christine down beneath the cellars of the Opera House.

She was glad the Phantom would not lie eternally in an unmarked grave—for the only place for the Phantom of the Opera to finally find peace would be near the music he loved only too well.